Lilac Blossom
Time

*Also by Carrie Bender
in Large Print:*

Birch Hollow Schoolmarm

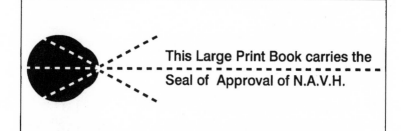

This Large Print Book carries the
Seal of Approval of N.A.V.H.

Dora's Diary
2

Lilac Blossom Time

Carrie Bender

Thorndike Press • Waterville, Maine

Library of Congress Control Number: 2002111644
ISBN 0-7862-4833-5 (lg. print : hc : alk. paper)

CPL 25.95 Yale Group

Lilac Blossom Time

Contents

Age Twenty

As Maad in Minnesota

May 20, Ascension Day

Dear Diary,
Here I am, a twenty-year-old schoolmarm, sitting on a mossy log by a tumbling brook, enjoying Mahlon Swartzentruber's ferny, green woods. I'm drinking in the sweet springtime beauties all around me, breathing in the delicious fragrant air, laden with the scent of growing things and blossoms. The cheery trill of birdsong surrounds me.

I have a small bouquet of lilacs pinned to my cape, and their fragrance is hauntingly sweet. Each time I bury my face in the blossoms, it brings back memories of Matthew — that he came back and was still the same kind friend. My heart rejoices. Someone once said of lilacs, "There is something ethereal about them, almost as if they were remembering something heavenly — some divine, sweet thing."

I feel as if the course of my life has been changed in the past week. For one thing, Matthew came back. Second, I promised to work as *Maad* (hired girl) for a family here this summer, instead of going home to *Mamm un Daed* (mom and dad) in Lancaster County, as I had planned.

Dear Matthew could stay for only a week. He had promised his employer to return and work for another year, much to his regret now that we have all our misunderstandings straightened out. All is forgiven and forgotten. Months of loneliness and doubt and missent mail are behind us. We plan to exchange letters regularly now that I have the right zip code. The months will go by fast, we hope.

Matthew is gone, to care for the horses on the Kendleton farm in California. Was it really just yesterday that he left? It seems longer — but I decided that if I keep busy, time will go faster. So when Owen and Lizzie Hershberger came to see me last night and wondered if I could work for them as *Maad* this summer, my answer was yes. I might as well put some roots down in this community. I am thinking that after we are married, Matthew will want us to live here in Minnesota.

These woods are sure a lovely spot. It wonders me why I never came back here before. I spy a patch of shy wild violets, bordered by curly young green ferns. The spring sunshine filters through the tender new green growth on the trees. There is a drift of mayflowers in a damp, mossy hollow on the other side of the gurgling brook, and the breeze stirring through the maiden-like wild birches makes me want to take deep, delicious breaths of its sweetness.

Was it on a spring day like this, on that first Ascension Day so long ago, that Christ went back up to heaven? But the splendors and beauties of heaven must be many times more glorious than anything we've ever experienced here on earth.

Time for me to go. Mahlons have invited me to dinner [noon meal], along with some more company, and I want to go and help get the meal ready.

May 30, Sunday Afternoon

This finds me settled in at Owen Hershbergers' place. Church was at Perry Hershbergers' farmhouse this forenoon. Later this evening, I plan to attend a singing

11

there. It's just a half mile from here, so it will be no problem for me to walk there and back.

Owen and Perry are brothers. Just this March, Owens moved out to this community, so I never had any of their children as my pupils. But in the week I've been here, I've gotten to know all twelve of them, from seventeen-year-old Milo, down to four-month-old Baby Mary. Their family arrived in a rare way: six boys were born first, then six girls.

They are a jolly and easygoing bunch, taking things as they come; I am delighted to be working for them. They are produce farmers, and Lizzie (age thirty-seven) wants to help outside in the vegetable fields this summer. That's why they needed a *Maad*.

I already feel at home here. Feenie (Lovina), age nine, is the oldest girl. Then it's Mattie, eight; Rosie, six (the freckle-faced one); Fannie, four; Lizzie, two; and Baby Mary. The boys are Milo, seventeen; Simon, sixteen; Ura, fifteen; Fernandis, thirteen; Owen Jr., twelve; and Jerry, eleven.

My job is doing the housework and caring for the little ones. I feel accepted as though I were really part of the family. I

12

think it's because they're such a happy-go-lucky household. Yes, there are heaps of work to be done. But having the mother of the family at home makes a world of difference. I do not feel nearly the strain and responsibility pressing me down as when I was working at Enos Millers', and Betty, the mother, was in the hospital.

Then too, there is a *Daadihaus* (grandparents' house) connected to this farmhouse. Lizzie's parents, Milo and Mattie, both close to eighty, live there. Mattie is on a wheelchair. We often see *Daadi* (grandpa) Milo taking her for a stroll whenever the weather is fine.

Some of Mattie's grandchildren call her *Voggel Mammi* (bird grandma) because she has a parakeet. They are a friendly, likable old couple — actually, the whole family is that way. I'm sure I'm going to like working here. At any rate, being busy will make the time go fast.

May 30, Sunday Evening

I just came back from paying Daadi Milo and Mammi Mattie a short visit. It was so inspiring. They are truly a grand old couple.

When I told them I like inspirational books, Mammi gave me an old, yellowed

13

copy of a book entitled *Gold Dust.* She said it's out of print. That's too bad because it's good for giving spiritual guidance in daily life.

The preface of the book says,

Many will much enjoy having this little collection on their table so they can take it up and dwell upon it. Thoughts that cheer and sustain people gain greater meaning through little stories, prayers, and biblical references. Shining examples of golden thoughts and golden deeds form a magnificent tapestry and priceless collection of references offering inspiration and direction for a richer and nobler life. Each page glows with words of courage and hope.

I must remember to copy some of it in my diary from time to time, so its thoughts become engraved in my heart. I count them as inspirational jewels.

Looking out the window, I see that a soft spring rain has begun to fall, bringing a shower of blossoms down from the pear tree. A pair of robins has built a nest in its branches, and Mr. Robin is sweetly singing while the Mrs. patiently sits on her nest.

I'm thankful to be in this huge farmhouse, where I can have a room of my own. That means a lot to me, both for my privacy and so I don't have to feel I'm crowding the family.

Ya (yes), well, before it's time to get ready for the singing, I should study the text we had at church today.

June 1

Today I had a letter from Matthew — the highlight of my week! He writes that he's crossing off each day on his calendar, each mark bringing him one day closer to coming home. Yet Matthew likes working on that horse and cattle farm, with thoroughbred horses and Brahma cattle. His job is taking care of the brood mares and helping to train the young horses.

It sounds very interesting. I wish I could be there, too. Oh, well, my job is interesting, too, even when the piecrust should be cut with an ax (smiles).

I made a bunch of rhubarb pies this morning. Four-year-old Fannie and two-year-old Lizzie pulled chairs up to the table to watch and help. I'd promised them each a piece of dough to use in making her own tiny pie. When I had the dough at just the right consistency and went to get the stack of pie plates, Lizzie, wanting to help, dumped in another cupful of water. I quickly poured it off, but I had to work more flour in then, which made the dough harder to handle.

At the dinner table, when eleven-year-old Jerry cut a piece of the pie, he complained, "My, I should have an ax to cut this crust." The big boys snickered, and I'm sure I blushed pink. Jerry's *Daed* reprimanded the poor boy, and he had to leave the table. But with fourteen others at the table, two pies disappeared fast even though the crust was hard.

Oh, dear, if I want to keep my eyes open any longer, I'd have to prop them open with toothpicks. I'll have to finish this later. Good night.

Guess how many eggs I fried for breakfast this morning. Over three dozen! They all eat two each, and some of the boys eat four each. That gallon pitcher of milk empties fast, too. It's good they live on a farm and produce most of their own food. They all are on the go from dawn to dusk, working hard, and it sure takes the grub to keep them going. I can't blame Lizzie for wanting a break, preferring to help outside for awhile.

Let's see, where did I leave off last night? I wanted to write about the scare I had when I was doing the laundry and had the youngest children in my care. They had set up their play kitchen on the back porch and were happily playing. When I was hanging out the first load, I was counting my blessings, feeling thankful that the old Maytag wringer washer engine had started so easily. It was looking to be such a fine, sunny, breezy day for drying all those heaps of laundry.

The girls were happily playing with their dolls when I heard terrified screams coming from the washhouse. Rushing in, I found Lizzie with her arm caught in the wringer, and a hysterical Fannie doing

17

most of the screaming. I quickly reversed the wringer. What a relief it was to find that her arm was still all in one piece and not broken, though some bruise marks were showing.

Lizzie had pulled the wagon beside the washing machine to stand on it. Yes, she's the one who is into everything and takes the most watching, just at the age when you shouldn't let her out of sight. Yet she's so cute, with her merry blue eyes and looking so mischievous.

Then yesterday afternoon when Mamm Lizzie was out helping with the planting, Baby Mary was sleeping and Fannie and Lizzie were happily playing in the sandbox. I decided that would be a good time to write to Matthew. I went into the *Sitzschtubb* (sitting room) with my stationery, sat on the big sofa, and pulled up the library table. I was all enthused about having a silent visit with him.

Before I had even half a sheet filled, I heard Fannie frantically calling me. I hurried outside, and Fannie told me anxiously that Lizzie was lost. Fannie said she had been busy making a farm in the sand and had not seen the two-year-old go anywhere. *Oh, Elend (misery)!* I thought. What if she wandered out to the road?

Luckily, my first place to search was in the barn. There she was in the stable, standing right underneath a driving horse, between the front and back legs, unaware of any danger. She was happily talking and singing to herself. Weak and trembling with fear, I didn't breathe easy until she was safe.

I guess that experience taught me a lesson: no more writing to Matthew in the middle of the day! It seems there's never a dull moment, and no time and no need to get *Heemweh* (homesickness) either.

June 3

Baby Mary is at such an adorable age, with her big blue eyes and a natural curl on top of her head. Maybe I shouldn't say natural; the girls love to wet her hair and brush it up into a topknot of hair like a Kewpie doll. After it dries, it stays that way. Mary is a very *gsund* (healthy) baby, too, so different from the colicky ones.

If there were nothing else for me to do, I could spend all my time caring for Mary and holding her. I dream of having my first little girl and even picked out a name for her — Lila Mae. Of course, my dreams call for her to be born at lilac blossom time!

Last week Mammi Mattie, over in the

other end of the house, had a few misfortunes. She ate some toadstools that Jerry brought to his grandparents. All three of them thought they were mushrooms. Daadi ate some but vomited right away. Mammi had to go to the hospital and have her stomach pumped out. For a few days she was quite sick, and we were all worried about her. But now she's all right again.

Then yesterday, Daadi Milo, with his usual loving devotion, was taking her for an outing in the wheelchair. Somehow or other, in trying to maneuver her off the walk, he upset the wheelchair and dumped her out on the grass.

We're so glad she was not hurt — nothing but her dignity, I suppose. Mamm Lizzie made the remark that they are getting old. Daadi has a birthday coming next week (his eightieth). His children and grandchildren plan to surprise him with eighty packages, allowing him to open just one package a day. Then in February, when Mammi has her eightieth, they will do the same for her.

Thinking of them reminded me of the book *Gold Dust* that they gave me. Maybe I can take the time to copy something tonight, not exactly word for word, so I'll call it my

Golden Gem for the Day

What sweet enjoyment to be able to shed
a little happiness around us!
What an easy and agreeable task it is to try
to render others happy.
I have but to give a cup of cold water
to one of Christ's little ones.
Yes, even so small a gift as that, given in
God's name,
may be of service.
It may even give the Christian
the right to hope for a reward in heaven.

June 4

Owen Jr. (age twelve) and I have a thing going. He constantly razzes me about the easy job I have, being able to lounge around in the cool house, while he is out toiling in the hot sunshine or crawling around on his hands and knees. Depending on what he's doing, he has to bend over until his back nearly breaks.

So today I made a bargain with Owen. If his mother gives him permission, I'll let him stay inside and watch Baby Mary while I take the little girls with me and work at his job. The last spring frostfree date is later here, so they don't plant as early as back home in Lancaster County.

21

Today that job happens to be planting tomatoes.

Daed Owen and Mamm Lizzie were planning to go to a produce meeting and gladly gave their permission. I think they were amused. The Mamm filled a bottle of supplemental formula for the baby and figured it should be all right.

I enjoyed my afternoon working out in the field with the rest of the family, as the boys were doing the managing. But I kept wondering (and worrying a bit) how Owen was making out in the house. He gave me quite a tale of woe when I went in to prepare supper [evening meal].

When Baby Mary woke from her nap, she was happily cooing and gurgling in baby language. He put on her shoes, and immediately she became fussy. Soon she began to cry in earnest, and he walked the floor with her, rocked her, and took her outside to the swing, but nothing helped. He tried to give her a bottle, but she wouldn't take it at all.

Poor Owen was about to bring her out to me when he thought of checking her diaper pins. They were closed. "What a relief," he said. Then he decided to take off her shoes and found the problem: her one toe was bent backward. Poor baby! After that she was all right for a while.

Later in the afternoon, after she'd had her bottle and he wanted to rock her to sleep, she was fussy and restless again. Finally he got the bright idea of putting on his mother's white *Kapp* (prayer covering), remembering that she likes to play with the covering strings with one hand and to suck her thumb with the other. That did it! She was contented then and fell asleep after a while.

I don't think Owen will want to switch jobs again, right away. As he says, he didn't like it all that much. I had to think of a story we had in our reading book when I went to school. A man complained that his wife had it so much easier than he did. So the wife suggested they trade jobs for a day.

I remember some of what happened. While the man was in the basement to get something, the pig went into the kitchen and upset the butter churn, spilling the cream and trying to slurp it off the floor. He kicked the pig so hard that it died. After he threw the pig out and mopped the floor, he went to the milk shed to find more cream so he could churn butter for dinner.

After he churned a bit, with the baby

crawling around on the floor, he remembered that the cow was still in the barn. The sun was already high, and he thought it was too far for him to take the cow down to the meadow. So he led her up onto their sod roof, where a nice crop of grass was growing. Since the house was against a steep hill, he put a plank across from the hill to the roof, for the cow to walk over and graze.

He was afraid the cow might fall off the roof and break her legs or her neck. So he tied one end of the rope to the cow's neck, slipped the other end down the chimney, and tied it around his leg. Then to make oatmeal, he hurried to boil water in the fireplace pot while he ground the oats. He was hard at it when the cow fell off the roof and dragged him halfway up the chimney, where he stuck upside down. The cow hung halfway down the outside wall.

The man's wife was out with the scythe, cutting hay with other mowers. She cut extra swaths across the field as she waited for her husband to call her to dinner, but he never called her. So she went home, saw the cow hanging there, and freed her by cutting the rope with the scythe. That let her husband fall down the chimney, banging his head into the porridge pot of hot water.

It was a hilarious tale that made the man look dumber than most husbands are. But it did bring out a lesson: the grass may look greener on the other side of the fence, but it isn't always so.

June 6, a No-Church Sunday

Feenie and Mattie planned for the family to have a picnic back in the woods near the big beaver dam. So with my help, they prepared gallons of meadow tea, several dozen sandwiches, and a salad. They wrapped cookies and cake and brought jars of peaches up from the cellar.

We girls carried everything down to the picnic spot. Then we went exploring until Mamm Lizzie and Daed Owen came with Baby Mary and the boys. It was a lot of fun and so refreshing to take the time to enjoy God's handiwork in nature.

This afternoon I paid Daadi Milo and Mammi Mattie a visit. They are so dear and good-natured to me, almost taking the place of Grandma Annie and Grandpa Dave back home. That reminds me, I have a whole bunch of letters to write yet today, to Grandma Annie and Grandpa Dave; to

Mamm, Daed, Sadie, and the boys; to Priscilla (my birth mother) and her family; and, most important, to Matthew.

But first of all, I'll glean something out of *Gold Dust* for copying. Mammi Mattie asked me today how I like it, and I told her how much I appreciate it.

Golden Gem for Today
How few of us would address God
this way each night:
Lord, deal with me tomorrow
as I have this day dealt with others.
I was harsh to some, and from malice or
to show my own superiority,
I exposed their failings.
From my pride or dislike,
I refused to speak to others.
One I have avoided; another I cannot like
because she displeases me.
Let us never forget that if we hold back
from showing kindness to someone,
we have not forgiven that person.
Sooner or later it will be done unto us
even as we have done unto them.

And now for the letter writing. Matthew's comes first, for it is the most delightful to write.

Heaps of work to be done, early and late, with peas and strawberries at their peak. But then, there are lots of helpers here, too. Fernandis complains of being "stiff as a board" from stooping so much to pick all that produce. The menfolk are busy in the field, mowing, raking, and baling hay. How I love the sweet scent of the freshly mown clover, especially in the morning.

Sixteen-year-old Simon was sent out to the field this morning with a team of mules, to rake one of the hayfields. Not long ago, he started *rumschpringing* (running around with the young people). Since it was Monday morning, I guess he was still sleepy. He raked for about an hour, then turned the mules around, ready for another round. Simon let the mules rest for a while as he went to lie down in the fencerow, intending to snooze for just a few minutes.

He fell into a deep sleep. At lunchtime, when the dinner bell rang, he didn't hear it, but the mules did. They headed for the barn, sideways across the field, not caring what crops they dragged down, while Simon slept on. Milo and Ura saw the mules come in and suspected that Simon was asleep. They went out with a half bucketful of cold water, found him fast asleep, as they had expected, and gave him a rude awakening.

It was all in fun, they claimed. At least Simon had his face already washed, ready for lunch. In this family, the children play a lot of pranks on each other. They try to trick each other, and then everyone has a hearty laugh. They sure are a lively bunch.

July 13

The fire sirens sounded out rather urgently today. When they came closer and closer and turned in at Perry Hershbergers' place, we were really alarmed. Later we heard that one of the boys and a mule had fallen into the manure pit while they were scraping the barnyard. They were rescued in time, with no harm done. But the rescue crew wouldn't have given much for their chances of living if they had been there much longer. Those gases are really toxic.

A few days ago, we had a scare here at our house, too. Baby Mary was rolling around the kitchen in her walker and tumbled down the cellar steps. Ura had gone down for something and had forgotten to close the door. He brought her up, pale and limp.

The parents took her to the doctor to have her checked out. By evening, they were able to bring her home again. What a relief to see Baby Mary with her usual rosy cheeks. Mamm Lizzie said that they were almost afraid to take her to the doctor, what with the recent case of Amish parents being accused of child abuse. How sad it would be to have your dear children taken from you and put into foster homes!

Golden Gem for Today
For the Christian,
the most exquisite happiness
and the highest degree of holiness
is to do some good that can be
known by none but God.
How sweet it is to have none
but God as witness.

August 1

We are busier than ever. String beans are yielding abundantly. Cantaloupes, watermelons, sweet corn, tomatoes, peppers, and so on will soon be ripe. A few weeks ago on our no-church Sunday afternoon, the three oldest girls and I went for a walk in the neighbor's woods.

We had a great time. The girls threw off their summer bonnets and shoes and stockings, and went squealing and splashing, wading in the creek. We found a patch of wildflowers and a bubbling spring by a bed of lacy green ferns, an ideal place to go for watercress next spring.

That evening Feenie complained of something on her back that was bothering her. When Mamm Lizzie checked it out, she found a tick! She grabbed a fine-point tweezers, grasped the tick right next to Feenie's skin, and gently pulled it straight out, all in one piece. Then she disinfected the bite spot and the tweezers.

About ten days later, a red ring appeared on Feenie's leg. Suspecting Lyme disease, Mamm Lizzie took her to the family doctor, who told her she must see a specialist in the city. Her appointment was today, and I was chosen to take her in. Lizzie had a headache and could watch the younger children but didn't feel up to going to the city. Daed Owen hitched old Dick to the *Dachweggeli* (roofed buggy), and the girls and I drove to town to get the bus.

I had never driven that horse before and wasn't ready when we met Willie Hershberger driving a white horse. Old Dick spooked and took us up over the bank, nearly upsetting the *Dachweggeli*.

On the way home, it had begun to rain. We met a trottin' buggy with the people on it holding a big umbrella. Once again, old Dick acted like a skittish colt, but we got home safely.

Feenie, Mattie, and Rosie, who had never been in the city before, nor had a bus ride, thought it was a great adventure — until we went into a store. A clerk saw the girls' bare feet, firmly ordered us out of the store, and pointed to a sign that said, "Shoes and shirts required." As we meekly filed out, I heard her saying, in disgust, "Barefooted!"

We tried another store to get the box of Premium saltine crackers for Mamm Lizzie. The clerk in there was kind and friendly. But after I had paid, she said, "I don't know what you are, but I know you're not Amish. I know the Amish make their own crackers."

I just smiled and replied, "We make our own crackers in the wintertime when it's not so busy."

Then, out on the sidewalk, another embarrassing thing happened. We passed a fat lady, and Rosie shrilled out, *"Guck selle*

Fraa ihr fette Beh (look at that woman's fat legs)."

The woman angrily snapped, "*Ya, guck yuscht* (yes, just look)! *Heid dei eege Bisness* (mind your own business)!"

She must have been one of the old-timers from that area who still knew Pennsylvania Dutch [German].

There was one bright spot to the day: Feenie does not have Lyme disease. She does have ringworm, something that is easily treated if taken care of right away. It is very contagious and can even be spread by cattle.

Whew! I'm tired tonight.

August 17

Today was Daed Owen's birthday, so Daadi Milo and Mammi Mattie were here for supper. Mammi brought along a cake she had made herself, working from her wheelchair, and some fresh peaches.

Daadi told us what happened when he took Mammi for her rolling walk this morning. They went out the road (there is hardly any traffic), and Tippy, the dog, just insisted on following them. Daadi tried to chase the dog back, but he refused to go and dutifully kept on following them.

Soon Mammi noticed that her hearing aid was missing. Somehow or other she had managed to lose it. They hunted in the wheelchair and along every inch of the way they had come but couldn't find a trace of it.

After they were back on the porch, Daadi sank into a porch rocker. Imagine their surprise when Tippy came and deposited the hearing aid on his knee. Apparently he had found it beside the road and had it in his mouth all the way. Smart dog!

Daadi told another story: "When I was a boy and they were putting away tobacco, a few neighbor boys came to help. One offered the other ten dollars if he would eat one of those big green tobacco worms, never thinking that he really would do it. But he did, and the other boy had to pay." Ugh!

September 18

According to the wooly worms, we'll have a mild winter. The goldenrods are bright yellow. People say the hickory nuts and acorns are scarce this year, too.

Seventeen-year-old Milo loves to tease me about all the letters I get from Matthew. I tell him that he doesn't know how many of my letters are from Mamm and Daed, Peter, Sadie, and Crist. Yet whenever he has the chance, he keeps on good-naturedly teasing me.

I tease him sometimes, too, for it's obvious that he's interested in dating Matthew's younger sister Anna Ruth. After he is a church member, I assume they will start dating.

Dear old diary, I guess you are wondering why you don't hear much about Matthew lately. It's because I have a separate journal just for him, and what is in it is a secret. Of course, I save his letters, too, and someday I'll show that secret journal to him. I'm counting the months now until he gets back.

October 5, Housecleaning Time

I had a scare this afternoon when doing fall cleaning in the girls' room. After Mary woke from her nap, I took her with me. She was happily playing in a corner where the girls have their dolls and crib. When I came back into the room from shaking the rugs over the upper porch railing, I noticed the baby eating something.

After dinner, Daadi had given the girls

each a pack of Smarties, and I figured she had found those. But I had to make sure. *Ei, yi, yi* (oh, oh dear)! Here in her hand, she had some pellets of mice poison, in a packet she had dragged from under the dresser. Badly frightened, I ran out to the field with her to find help.

Daed Owen immediately went with me to the neighborhood phone shanty, three hundred feet from the house, to call the poison control center. They needed to know the age and weight of the child, the name of the product, and how much of it she ate. I reported that she didn't eat much because I emptied her mouth as soon as I saw what was happening.

The experts advised us to give her all the fluids we can. We are to watch for black-and-blue spots on her and for any injury that might not stop bleeding.

Baby Mary seemed to be okay and was her usual sunny self for the rest of the day. Oh, what a relief! She does a lot of crawling around and exploring. Tonight she brought me a handful of orange and gold marigolds from the planter on the porch. They had not yet succumbed to Jack Frost. I gave her a hug in return!

I sure will miss them all when I leave here!

Golden Gem for Today

Take these simple counsels for a young girl
and let them sink deep into your heart,
as the dew sinks into the flower:
Distrust the love that comes too suddenly.
Distrust the pleasure that
fascinates too keenly.
Distrust the words that trouble or charm.
Distrust the book that gives you
wild dreams.
Distrust the thought that
you cannot confide
to your mother.

The last one stirs within me the longing to have a face-to-face and heart-to-heart talk with my own dear Mamm. For now, I'll have to be satisfied with letters.

October 25

Tonight I went for a walk in the dusky twilight, as tranquil evening shadows fell over fields of corn stubble. The sun was going down in a maze of red and gold. Then a silvery full moon slowly rose in the night sky. Far away, a coyote howled, sending shivers up and down my spine.

I feel so sorry tonight for the Ezra Lambright family. Their little four-year-old daughter has leukemia. The treatments were making her so sick that they decided to stop them and try some alternate natural treatment. But the officials decided otherwise. When the parents failed to bring the child for the appointments, child welfare workers took her away from her parents and put her into foster care so she could have the needed treatments. How disruptive for the family! I hope the child recovers soon and can go home.

This afternoon I heard Daadi Milo puttering around in the shop, so I went out to see what he was up to. He had one shoe off and said, "I dropped a frying pan on my toe this morning. I have such awful pain and pressure under my toenail. I've endured it long enough. Now I'm going to drill a small hole in the toenail to relieve the pressure."

I begged him not to do that and to see a doctor instead, but he paid me no heed. So I went out to get Daed Owen. When I reached the driveway, I saw a runaway team of horses come galloping in through the field with a wagonload of broccoli. The broccoli heads were flying out in all directions. The team did not stop till they'd reached the barn. Then we had a grand broccoli-picking-up party.

After the job was finished and I was walking back to the house, I remembered Daadi's toe. I went into their part of the house. Daadi had a big smile on his face as he reported that his pain and pressure in the toe were instantly relieved after he drilled the hole. Well, well! I surely don't recommend such self-treatment!

November 1

The work here is beginning to taper off, leaving more time for diary writing. I'm beginning to wonder what's next for me. I really won't be needed here at Hershbergers' this winter, though Lizzie said I'm perfectly welcome to stay and work on things for my hope chest, if I wish.

I would like to piece and quilt a dahlia pattern for one bedspread and maybe quilt several others, and then embroider some pillowcases. But I could do that back home with Mamm and Daed, if there was a way to go to Pennsylvania with a party traveling in a van.

Wedding season is here, decorated by snow flurries. In one of Matthew's last letters, he wondered if I would agree to have a spring wedding instead of a November wedding, as customary among our people.

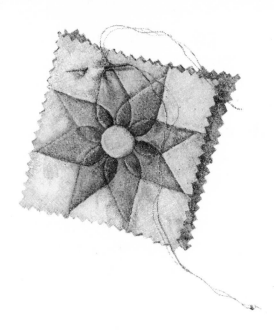

His term of employment ends in the spring. I wrote back that it's fine with me. So he has written to the bishop in my district in Lancaster County to see if he would be willing to marry us in the spring. Now I'm anxiously awaiting Matthew's reply.

Yesterday fifteen-year-old Ura had a rough time. He went to the mill with a two-mule wagon and brought back a load of feed for the cows: bags of gluten, bran and middlings, ground oats, and cotton-seed meal. Ura drove the loaded wagon and the team of mules up the barn bank and into the second floor of the old part of the barn, as instructed by his dad. He was about to empty out the bags on a pile on the barn floor so the brothers could mix it with a shovel.

Just then, with creaks and groans and splintering wood, the supporting beams of the old floor gave way. Mules, wagon, feed sacks, and all fell down to the floor below. Ura was stunned, and his arm hung at a grotesque angle, so Daed Owen summoned an ambulance. Now Ura is at home again, with his arm in a cast, but he is not much hurt otherwise. We have a lot to be thankful for.

Golden Gem for Today
Grant me my temporal blessings — clothing, nourishment, shelter —
but not too much of anything;
and let me have the happiness
of sharing my blessings
with those poorer than myself today.
Grant me the blessing of intelligence
so I can understand golden counsels
that lift the soul
and lend wings to the thoughts.

November 16

Oh, how I will miss this family when I must leave. They take me as their big sister, and I think Baby Mary takes me for her mother. I wish I'd have had time to write down more of the little ones' cute antics and the funny things that happened. Maybe I could still record a few of them, such as the time the little girls decided to go fishing.

They sneaked Jerry's fishing line and had actually put a worm on the hook. Then a big rooster came out from the barnyard, spied this worm going by, and pounced on it, swallowing hook and all.

Ach, mei (oh, my), such a fuss and tears when they saw what they had caught! We ended up butchering the rooster and eating him for supper. Jerry was upset that they had used his fishing line without his permission. "Be sure your sins will find you out!"

Mamm Lizzie told me about another amusing thing that happened shortly before I came here. Early in the morning, before anyone else was up, a little freckle-faced girl crept quietly down the stairs, softly opened the door, and ran out. She was headed for the meadow, dotted with buttercups and forget-me-nots, where the dew lay heavy on the grasses.

There was a chorus of birdsong, but she probably didn't even hear it because she was too intent on accomplishing her mission. Just before she had gone to bed, Jerry had told her that on the first of May, if you go and wash your face in the dew before sunrise, before you speak one word to anyone, your freckles will disappear.

Imagine Rosie's dismay when, as she ran down the orchard path, she met cousin Wallie Hershberger coming up the path with a note for Mamm Lizzie. He spoke to her. She knew it would be rude not to reply, so she answered him. Then she promptly burst into tears, thinking she had lost her chance to get rid of her freckles for another year.

Poor bewildered Wallie wondered what he had done to make her cry. When the story reached Mamm Lizzie's ears, she, in her motherly wisdom, reassured Rosie that freckles were nice and nothing to be ashamed of. Then she put a stop to Jerry's teasing.

I'm longing for the beauties of May right now, when the lovely lilacs bloom and the spring rains fall, when the tulips bloom and, best of all, when Matthew comes home. But longing won't help. It's still a half year away.

November 25, Thanksgiving Day

Well, I guess there won't be any spring wedding after all. The bishop replied that if a wedding is for a widow or widower, the practice is to perform it any time of year. While he won't actually forbid it, the ministers around Lancaster encourage young people to get married in November, following the usual custom.

I know this might be different in other Amish settlements, and even the bishop out in this Minnesota district likely would not mind. But we want to respect my home bishop's wishes since he will be performing the ceremony.

Oh, well, good things are worth waiting for, I'm sure, and Owens will probably give me a job again next summer. They're talking of putting up a big greenhouse sometime.

Baby Mary walked alone for the first time today, when some of the Hershberger *Freindschaft* (relatives) were here for a Thanksgiving meal. Everyone cheered her for the new achievement. She looks so tiny and so young to be able to manage it. Baby Mary seems to grow sweeter every day, and I will miss her terribly when I leave here. She's my little girl. In fact, I think she takes me more for her mother than she does Mamm Lizzie.

There's an old-fashioned, wintry blizzard starting outside, and it's bitterly cold.

The roads will probably be blown shut by morning. So much for the mild winter they had predicted!

Golden Gem for Today
Joy in life is like oil in a lamp.
When the oil gets low,
the wick is consumed,
sending up a black vapor.
A life without joy passes away without profit,
shedding around it only gloom and sorrow.
If we open our hearts to heaven,
as we open our windows to the sun and air,
God will fill us with a calm,
sweet joy that elevates the soul.

December 2

The community had a benefit sale yesterday for Ezra Lambrights, to help with their hospital bills. Their little girl has not yet been returned to them. I'm sure that many a prayer has been sent heavenward on their behalf, both for the strength and courage to bear it and for her return.

At the benefit sale, people sold several hundred subs and buffaloburgers, plus lots of baked goods. They made the burgers right there at the sale. There was a long waiting line. Ezra's dog got in line, too.

Every time the line moved forward, he also moved. When his turn came, the clerk rewarded him with a free burger. Smart dog!

We, meaning Owens, bought Ezra's airtight kitchen range to replace the worn-out Warm Morning stove they had in the kitchen. The boys set up the new range right away. Last night before bedtime, Daed Owen put coal in the stove and banked the fire for the night. Not long after everyone was in bed, there was a terrific poof! Quite an explosion. The stovepipe running through the boys' room was blown off, clattering to the floor and strewing soot and ashes all over.

Owen's brother Perry told him that he likely cut the draft off too soon, before the stove was hot enough, and it created gases without proper combustion. I guess Owen has to learn how to care for that stove.

Strangely, it didn't even wake up the little ones. But the boys had quite a time cleaning their room in the middle of the night.

The joyous Christmas season is fast approaching. If only Matthew could be here!

I received a big box by UPS today, an early Christmas gift from Matthew. It was a lovely handcrafted silverware chest. As a labor of love, Matthew had made it himself, in his spare time, using his boss's tools. Inside of the chest I found his Christmas card and letter, which I shall always treasure and keep. Now I must hurry and send off my letter to him.

I made Matthew a shirt, following the pattern his sister Rosabeth was kind enough to loan me. I also bought him a Bible and had his name engraved on the leather cover. I hope he receives it in time.

I was beginning to wonder if we would have a green or brown Christmas. Now we finally have about nine inches of snow covering the fields. The roads aren't drifted shut yet, and there is enough snow and ice on the road for traveling by horse and sleigh.

Tonight the youth of *rumschpringing* age went Christmas caroling on a big bobsled. They stopped in here for hot chocolate and cookies. Milo and Anna Ruth are dating now, and they make an ideal couple.

After the carolers had gone on to the next farmhouse, Daed Owen and Mamm

Lizzie were in a reminiscing mood tonight. We all sat around the table, sipping hot chocolate and nibbling on cookies.

Owen told of the time he and Lizzie had their first date. He teased her good-naturedly: "When I was coming into your parlor for the first time, you were so flustered that you greeted me at the door, not realizing you were still wearing your old, rundown milking shoes. When you finally did notice them, you gasped and blushed as pink as a rose — like a real bride-to-be.

"Another time, a mouse ran across the parlor and disappeared under the sofa, scaring you. Before you realized what you were doing, you were up on a chair, stifling a scream! That gave me a chance to rescue you."

Lizzie had things to tease him about, too: "Remember the time you spilled a pitcher of cream at a wedding? Then once someone moved a chair just as you were about to sit down, and you sat on the floor instead. What a laugh all the young people had!"

The children thought it was great fun hearing these things and begged for more. I hope someday to have a house full of children just as dear and precious as these. I sure will miss them all when I leave.

Golden Gem for Today
Let us cultivate carefully and
joyously the portion of soil
Providence has committed to our care.
To do well what is given to us
is all that God requires from our hands.
Happy is the approval of conscience
that whispers,
"You have done as Christ would have done."

December 25, Christmas Day

I can still hardly believe it that I really am home! One week ago today, I found out that a vanload was heading for Pennsylvania and that there was room for one more passenger. It was one of the best Christmas gifts I ever received.

I got to celebrate Christmas Day with Mamm, Daed, Peter, Sadie, Crist, Henrys, Rudys, and Grandpa Daves. That was wonderful. My, how the children have grown!

There was the usual stuffed roast turkey and gravy, heaps of fluffy mashed potatoes and vegetables, including corn, golden filling, and the usual array of desserts, Christmas cookies, and candies. I spent the afternoon playing games with the children. At the same time, I tried to listen in on the adult conversation.

Sadie is prettier and more rosy cheeked than ever, and sporting such a sweet, charming personality. I suspect that she will soon be spoken for, and blessed will be the lad who claims her.

I spent the evening writing to Matthew, and now I'm too tired to write more. How luxurious it will feel to be in my own soft, comfortable bed again, without a care to mar my dreamless sleep.

December 27

Well! I guess I've landed myself a job, ready or not. I still have my doubts about it, but I've consented to give it a try. This afternoon a shiny, expensive-looking car pulled into our drive, and an elderly lady, assisted by a young man, came to our porch door.

Mamm welcomed the visitors to come in out of the cold. The son helped his mother to the sofa.

She introduced herself as Ophelia Worthington and her son as Grant Worthington. They were old friends of Gloria Graham, who used to be our neighbor but now lives in Arizona. Gloria had advised them to come here and said she was sure they wouldn't be turned away.

Then Mrs. Worthington came right out with her request. She wants a sweet young plain girl to be her companion for six weeks while her personal maid recuperates from surgery.

I thought of Sadie, who would perfectly fit that description. But Mamm turned questioning eyes to me, saying, "Sadie has promised to help a family with a new baby in a week or two."

Just as I was starting to say that I'm sure I don't fit into her requirements, her son interrupted me: "I do a lot of traveling and am hardly ever at home. My mother has other maids to do the cleaning and cooking, and a butler and a gardener besides. She just wants a fill-in helper until her maid recovers."

Mrs. Worthington said, "You would be able to do handwork, even piecing and quilting for your hope chest, maybe, while you sit with me."

I think what she really wants is a friend to talk to. She said her other maids are stiff and haughty and not very sociable. I had to wonder if maybe she's a bit hard to please. Oh, well, if I can't please her, we can call it quits anytime.

I just hope I didn't bite off more than I can chew. Maybe it will even be rather pleasant. Mamm told me, "If it turns out not to be a desirable or pleasant place, for any reason, you can come flying back home immediately." That's good to know.

I think Mamm was worried about the worldly environment and surrounding luxuries, but I don't think they will affect me. I'm apprehensive and excited at the same time. On New Year's Day, I leave for Winslow Manor, their mansion, for better or for worse.

Golden Gem for Today
The Christian should be like a wayside spring, giving refreshment from the fountain of life. We provide a place where the weary traveler stoops to drink and share cheering smiles and comforting words. We protect and nourish others, like the tree whose branches offer fruit and shade for all.

As Companion for Mrs. Worthington

January 1, New Year's Day

Today has been a long day, my first one as helper for Mrs. Worthington. Yes, I feel that she is rather demanding and exacting, but maybe I shouldn't be so quick to judge. After all, she wasn't feeling well, and the day was probably as hard for her as it was for me.

She likes to stay in bed till ten in the morning, skipping breakfast. Her lunch is supposed to be at one o'clock, and dinner (what I call supper) at seven. Then she watches TV until late (she's at it right now), so I have plenty of time to myself.

I explored the whole house. It was a grand old mansion when it was built, over

175 years ago, but by now it needs a lot of repairs. The paint is peeling off the high ceilings, and in some places the plaster is crumbling. But the furnishings are elegant, and the carpets are plush.

Fireplaces are spread all over the house. The biggest one is in the library, where Clark, the butler and chauffeur, keeps a cheery blaze going all the time. He's not really a butler, but I suppose he was one day, and the name has stuck. Clark is the handyman around here — a cheerful and friendly old man with grizzled hair. When I see him puttering around the house at odd jobs, whistling a tune or humming to himself, I think of George Washington Carver, for he is of that color.

I haven't gotten to know the maids at all. As far as I can see, they're just as Mrs. Worthington described them — stiff and haughty, and prim and proper. I'm the only young person in the house, unless you'd count Grant when he's here. He must be in his upper thirties already. This morning when Clark came for me, in his ancient but well-cared-for Cadillac, he told me that Grant is vacationing in the Bahamas just now and won't be back for several weeks.

Now let me describe my room. It's large,

and my bed is a four-poster with a canopy overhead. There are four high windows, with thick, heavy drapes that you open and close by pulling cords. On the walls are old paintings with gold frames and a big, cracked mirror. There's a wide fireplace with a stone mantle, but it's not in use, yet my room is cozy warm. So I suppose there's oil heat in addition to the fireplaces.

A big oval braided rug covers most of the hardwood floor, and there's a desk and a soft easy chair, plus the dresser and wardrobe. The desk is just the thing for diary writing. But right now, the bed looks mighty inviting to me. I've been up since five o'clock this morning, and that's nearly half a day before Mrs. Worthington gets up. She probably watches television till long after midnight, hours after I am in dreamland.

I've brought along a stamped cross-stitch quilt top to embroider, for I don't think I could stand doing nothing. Idleness is the devil's workshop anyway, as the saying goes.

January 2

Mrs. Worthington was feeling a lot better today. Now I realize that yesterday I formed an entirely wrong opinion of her. She's a

55

good sport and not at all hard to please. I suppose most people, when they aren't feeling well, seem demanding and exacting.

Today she talked quite a bit, and guess what! She stems from Quaker heritage! Up until 1932, her people dressed plain: the men wore broad-rimmed black hats, and the woman wore long dresses and bonnets, probably much like we still do today. They said "thee"and "thou" instead of *you*.

Mrs. Worthington hasn't stayed in the old faith, but nevertheless she says she is a Christian. She told me some about Quaker services and beliefs, which were quite interesting to me. They have no ordained preachers. Whoever feels inspired to talk gets up and speaks to the group. There are times of just silence and meditation, too.

At Quaker weddings, there's no bishop to perform the ceremony. The couple just gets up and says their vows to each other in front of the congregation. Then everyone signs their name on a ledger, affirming that they were witnesses to the taking of the vows.

One tidbit of information especially amused me. It used to be a custom of the Quakers to appoint someone with a feather in his hand to watch for anyone falling asleep in church. If someone did, they were to go and tickle his nose to awaken him! That might be a good idea for in our services, too!

Mrs. Worthington told me that a conscientious man, George Fox, started the Quaker movement. He had a lot of followers, called The Society of Friends. The English government persecuted them.

Once, when George was brought before a magistrate, he refused to remove his hat. Instead he told the officer, "I bid thee tremble before the word of the Lord."

The judge snapped back, "I bid you to quake before the word of the law."

Right then and there, the Society of Friends got the new name "Quakers." William Penn was a Quaker, and I guess most everyone knows that Pennsylvania got its name from Penn's Woods. Penn founded Philadelphia, the city of brotherly love, and did much to keep peace with the Indians.

Oh! There goes Mrs. Worthington's bell. I suppose she's tired of watching TV and wants someone to talk to.

January 3

The sun went down behind the ridge just west of here, leaving a trail of glorious rose and pink-tinted clouds. The scene reminded me that I haven't been out of doors since I came here. Tomorrow morning, before Mrs. Worthington awakens, I hope to bundle up, take a walk outside in the snow, and do some exploring. I've already done two patches on my quilt, but I sure miss getting exercise.

This morning I was up early, before anyone else was up (or so I thought) and decided to do some more exploring in this big old mansion. The library has shelves and shelves of volumes of big, heavy, and ancient books that don't appear to be the least bit interesting.

The drawing room (*Sitzschtubb*, we would say) has interesting antique furnishings and is the most elegant room in the house. Mrs. Worthington told me that Clark has a workshop in the basement, where he spends most of his spare time in the winter. I decided to snoop around down there, to see what he makes. He was in his shop before me. With a hearty, welcoming voice, he invited me to come in, sit on a stool, and visit with him.

Clark had a block of wood in one hand and a carving knife in the other. He was whittling some intricate thing. The shelf above his worktable contains things he's already made, and they're really good! The one I liked best was a stagecoach drawn by four horses, looking so real and lifelike. They're painted too, down to every little detail, harnesses, and all.

I was rather lavish with my praise. Clark was pleased, and I suppose, like everyone else in this house, lonely for someone to talk to. He was telling interesting stories of long ago, stuff about the history of this mansion. Clark asked, "Did Mrs. Worthington tell you that this place was once an Underground Railroad station?"

She had not, and I couldn't believe it, so he showed me a little room in the basement that no one would suspect is there. A panel in the wall slides back to reveal it, and he said there is even an underground tunnel from the old carriage house to this little room. He opened the trapdoor in the floor and showed me the steps leading down into it.

Clark's great-great-grandfather stayed in that room for two days after he ran away from his master and was on his way to Canada. Mrs. Worthington's great-great-grandparents, who were Quakers, operated the Underground Railroad station. They were kind and helped many people of color to escape slavery.

There are several more secret rooms in this house, which Clark promised to show me sometime. He appreciated having an audience and nearly got carried away with his storytelling, sharing things handed down by his great-great-grandparents. These were stories of daring escapes from slaveholders, wading through streams so the slave hunters' bloodhounds couldn't follow their scent, hiding in the woods, buried beneath underbrush by day, and traveling by night.

Sometimes they traveled in the beds of wagons belonging to conductors of the Underground Railroad (often Quakers). They would hide under mounds of straw and sometimes under sacks of potatoes and onions. The fugitives learned to follow the North Star and to signal to each other, using the call of a hoot owl or a whippoor-will.

When he first stepped across the border into the promised land of Canada, one of the slaves said, "It feels like heaven's shore, and the glory-light shines all around me."

It was all so interesting. Sometime I must ask Mrs. Worthington more about her great-great-grandparents who once lived in this very house.

It's time for bed. I'm glad to say that yesterday's homesick feeling is gone. No longer do I need to keep "counting the days till Sunday." I think I'll take the time to copy an inspirational verse yet.

Golden Gem for Today

A young girl, in one of those moments
when the heart seems to overflow
with devotion,
wrote in her journal:
"If I dared, I would ask God why
I am placed in the world, and
what I have to do.
If only I might but do some
good to another."
A few days later, she reread those
lines and thought,
"Why, nothing is easier! Even little things
like a kind word,
a little vexation patiently borne,
a prayer for a friend offered to God,
the fault or thoughtlessness of another repaired
without his knowledge —
God will recompense it all a thousandfold."

January 4

I was up early for my planned morning walk in the snow. Again Clark had arrived first and was already shoveling snow off the walks when I stepped outside. Last night's fresh snowfall added about four inches. He called a cheery greeting to me, and his big, black Lab dog came bounding over to me, wagging his tail, glad for a chance for a romp, I suppose.

We walked to the ridge west of the house, where there's a stand of spruces, and even saw some wildlife. Two rabbits bounded away. Lots of birds were in view: chickadees, nuthatches, snowbirds, tufted titmice, and two cardinals. I must ask Mrs. Worthington whether she'd mind if I put up a bird feeder outside the library window. It wouldn't be hard to attract all kinds of beautiful birds here. But maybe she wouldn't like to have the drapes opened. I think that's one of the first things I'd like to do in this house — let the sun shine in!

I came back with rosy cheeks and was actually hungry for breakfast. That is a good feeling. Ever since I've been here, what with not working hard like I was used to doing, I was never hungry when meal-times came around. Exercise sure makes me feel a lot better!

I was ready for another day of waiting on Mrs. Worthington. She wants her back rubbed, her pillows rearranged, a shawl for her shoulders (either to be put on or taken off every fifteen minutes or so), some warm water for soaking her feet, and then a foot massage. I also have to see that she takes about six or eight different prescription medicines. Sometimes she wants to doze, and other times she might feel like talking.

Mrs. Worthington has a lot of worries about her son Grant, her only child. According to her, he lives his life in idleness and vanity. He has never had to work and is still doing much carousing and partying. She has hopes that someday he will settle down and even marry yet and give her some grandchildren. She does not talk about the state of his soul. I imagine that his ancestors, pious Quakers, would be horrified at his loose living.

I must write to the dear ones at home yet. I should have done it earlier. One nice thing about this job — there's plenty of time to write long letters to Matthew! I don't send him a letter every day, but I do write a few words to him nearly every day. When the sheet's about half as long as my arm, I send it off. There's no one here to tease me about the letters I write and receive, either!

I told Mrs. Worthington today about Matthew and our plans to get married when he comes home. She was quite interested and asked a lot of questions about our customs and weddings and clothing. When I told her we don't wear bridal gowns and veils, and that I'll just wear a plain dress made just like the one I'm wearing now, she was really surprised and thought it's a pity.

She said I ought to go up to her attic sometime and look into a certain chest and see all the bridal finery she wore on her wedding day. She gave me permission to look through all the trunks up there, if I wish, and bring down anything that interests me, even old letters. Wow! I sure look forward to that, with the rich history this mansion has.

Her great-great-grandmother, as a young Quaker girl, had traveled out West in a covered wagon and married out there. Eventually she received word that a rich bachelor uncle who had just died had willed her this estate, a large farm at that time. So she and her husband returned east, to this very place, and later built this elaborate (for that time) mansion.

There were acres and acres of land, big

barns, and carriage houses. The rich uncle had made his fortune in the ironworks. He had had a sweetheart at one time. He had planned to build a house for her, but she jilted him. So he lost interest in the estate and traveled out West himself.

Mrs. Worthington's great-great-grandmother's name was Idella McNeil Davis. After building this house, she and her husband became active in helping to free the slaves by Underground Railroad, and this house was a station. Whew! If this house could talk, it would surely have a lot of interesting stories to tell! I can hardly wait to explore those old trunks in the attic.

January 10

Back again, after being at home over Sunday, which had been part of our agreement. I don't often attend the singings anymore, but last night I did and enjoyed the music!

This morning Clark came for me in the Cadillac. On the way back, snowflakes began to fall in earnest, along with blizzard winds. It's been snowing and blowing all day, a real, old-fashioned blizzard; all the roads are blown shut.

It seems like a luxury to have all the rooms here so cozy warm, even though the winds are howling around the corners of the house. At our home, the rooms are icy cold, all except the big kitchen, the hub of all activity, heated by the big black cookstove. When company comes, we also light the stove in the *Sitzschtubb* (sitting room).

Mrs. Worthington wasn't feeling the best today, and so I didn't get a chance to explore the attic yet. Tonight I'm entirely too tired, but I will take the time yet to copy something out of my devotional book.

Golden Gem for Today
We nourish the soul with —
Pious thoughts, read, meditated upon,
and sometimes written.
Books that elevate and instill love
for all that is good and holy.
Conversations that refresh, rejoice, and cheer.
Walks that expand the mind and
strengthen the body.

January 11

The world around us is a place of indescribable beauty today, with the deep drifts and swirls of beautiful snow. The wind had stopped this morning by the time I got up. I helped Clark shovel snow, clearing off the porches and walkways. He told me where I could find a pair of snowshoes, and I had time for an exhilarating walk before it was time to go in to attend to Mrs. Worthington.

She was much better today, so she gave me permission to explore the attic while she rested after lunch. I'm excited about what I found! There were a lot of really old-fashioned clothes, including Mrs. Worthington's wedding finery, old letters, and greeting cards. But nothing interested me like what I found wrapped up in an old silk hoop-skirted gown: Idella McNeil's journal!

The journal begins with her, along with her parents, brothers and sisters, starting on their journey to the wild and unknown West! I didn't have time to read much of it yet, but it looks to be tremendously interesting. The last entry she made said, "The war is over now, and the slaves are freed at last."

Maybe if I search the attic some more, I'll find a few more of her journals, or perhaps she had only one. It covered about fifteen years of her life, so she must have written only the highlights. Mrs. Worthington told me she has read it over several times years ago. She gave me permission to read it, then I'm to take it down to her. Perhaps I'll even copy a bit of her story in my journal, as part of my memories of living here with Mrs. Worthington.

The journal is very old: the pages are brittle and yellowed, and some are loose. If I were Mrs. Worthington and would have a journal written by my great-great-grandmother, I think I'd have it recopied and bound into a book. Even now it's already rather difficult to make out the words; I really have to concentrate. Maybe tomorrow I can make some more headway.

January 12

From where I'm sitting here at the desk, I can see out the window to a place on a hill, probably about two miles away. There are lights in all the windows. For some reason it reminds me of our farmhouse at home. It gives me a bit of *Heemweh* (homesickness) to think of them all happily gathered in our big, cozy kitchen. Dad would be reading the farm paper, Mamm hooking a rug, Sadie doing hand sewing, Peter working on his grandfather's clock kit, and Crist helping him and watching.

Then I think of Matthew and wonder

what he's doing tonight. Writing a letter to me, I hope. I wish I could go and visit him, to see what the farm is like where he works, and see the horses and cattle. He has written so much about it in his letters that I can almost see it in my mind's eye.

Today Mrs. Worthington had another not-so-well day, and I'm too tired tonight to tackle that old journal. I'm feeling a little blue and *Heemweh* tonight. Maybe copying something from *Gold Dust* will encourage me.

Golden Gem for Today
What wonders are wrought by
an act of loving-kindness!
Jesus himself is glorified thereby,
and he sheds abundant grace upon us.
Our guardian angel sees us,
listens, draws nearer,
and makes us feel that we have done right.
The angels above experience a sudden joy
and look upon us tenderly.

January 16

I've spent these last several evenings reading Idella McNeil's journal and finally finished it. For awhile, I could hardly lay it down. Tonight I took it down to Mrs. Worthington. She wanted to reread it and for once had something better to do than watch television. However, she strained her poor eyes while trying to decipher those yellowed old pages. She wants me to read it aloud to her, at least part of it every day. And she even wants me to copy it, for those doubtful future grandchildren!

Mrs. Worthington wants it handwritten, not typed, so it looks more authentic and like the original journal. It will be quite an undertaking, I'm afraid. I guess I'll have to put on hold my project of filling my hope chest. Oh, well, I'm working for her and must do as she says.

January 17

The Worthington household is in a dither: Master Grant is coming home in two days! The cleaning maids are going all out to thoroughly clean each room. The cook is outdoing herself in making gourmet dishes. Mrs. Worthington has called in some kind of a hairdresser or whatever you call her, who is carefully grooming her pompously coifed hair and even her artistically painted fingernails.

I never thought that such a homecoming for a ne'er-do-well son would create such a sensation. But after all, he is her son, and I suppose the servants are just following orders. The last time he was here, around Christmas, was just for a day. They had not known he was coming, but now they have the privilege of preparing for him. I don't exactly look forward to it, but Mrs. Worthington is really excited.

She says we'll read aloud from Idella McNeil's journal after Grant has left, but she wants to show it to him. She thinks he will be immensely interested in it. I have a feeling that I'll never see it again after he has it in his hands. Oh, well, I must not feel that I have any claims to it just because I enjoyed reading it. Time for bed. It's supposed to be a big day tomorrow.

January 18

Mrs. Worthington is feeling down in the dumps because Grant didn't show up. He sent word that he will be here a week from today instead. Clark was keenly disappointed, too.

I've been spending my mornings sitting on a stool in Clark's whittling shop, appliquéing Rose Garden quilt patches. Now both those and the embroidered patches are finished, and I'm ready to start working on recopying the old journal. Years ago, Clark read it, too, and wants to reread it when I'm finished copying it. He seems to like my company and was delighted when I asked whether he minds if I work on the journal in his shop, too.

Clark is a kindhearted and interesting old man. I get awfully lonely sitting alone in my big room, with the portraits of those McNeil ancestors looking down on me, disapprovingly, it sometimes seems.

Clark has told me a lot more about this Underground Railroad station. He could search far and wide and not find a more keenly interested listener than I am. I wish I could write it all down in my diary. Today he also talked a lot about Grant and his disappointments in him. Mr. Worthington (Grant's dad) died when Grant was only two years old, and Clark took the place of a dad to him then, before he was sent off to boarding school.

According to Clark, he had been a fine, good-hearted, promising lad, following Clark around everywhere. Clark did his best to teach him right from wrong and told him many Bible stories. But sadly, Grant fell in with bad companions during his teen years. That was combined with having all the money he wanted to spend, however he pleased, and not having to work. It all was the ruination of him, according to Clark.

Yet Clark has said that every day he's praying for Grant, that he will give up his bad habits yet, give his life to Christ, become a person of worth, and make a contribution to some worthy cause.

Golden Gem for Today
Listen to God.
Be attentive to God's counsels and warnings.
God speaks to us in gospel words that come to
our minds and in the good thoughts that
suddenly dawn upon us. We hear God's voice
in the devout words that meet us
in some book, on a sheet of paper,
or falling from the lips of a preacher, a friend,
or even a stranger.

January 19

I'm making good progress in copying Idella McNeil's journal. Mrs. Worthington asked to have it tonight to read over what I've already done, so I can't work on it now. She's feeling quite well these days and eagerly looking forward to her son's arrival next week. I hope she won't be disappointed again.

I find that I'm missing Idella tonight (the very idea!). I feel as if I'm getting to know her through her writings. She had dreams and hopes and fears, just like the young girls of today do. The fact that she was a Quaker girl endears her to me. She too wore a bonnet and a long plain dress and apron. But then, I guess most country people did in those days. I don't suppose anyone wore miniskirts or shoes with spike heels, or put on makeup, or had glamorous hairdos (smiles).

I don't have any material or thread here to start another quilt before I go home for the weekend, and I must have something to do tonight. I got the notion of copying the outline of Idella's story in my diary. By now I know it by heart. She wrote about their long journey westward in covered wagons, with her parents, four sisters, and three brothers, when she was eighteen.

Panthers, bears, and wolves were still in the forests. They faced dangers from swollen rivers, bad storms, and quicksand, cholera, and fever. Yet those first journal entries were bright with hope. Most Indians were peaceable. Early wildflowers along the trail were in bloom, and the birds were singing.

The family cow was tied behind the

wagon. They had a crate of hens along. It must've been exciting at first, stopping to make camp every night, visiting with other travelers around campfires, singing, and playing the harmonica. They slept under the stars if the weather was fine, listening to coyotes howling from the hills.

After a while, though, it became tiresome. To stretch their legs, they took turns walking. Each family had a watchdog along to warn them of danger and thieving varmints. The dogs trotted under the wagons, knowing enough to keep away from the wheels. The men carried their rifles, watching for small game. They made side trips into the woods with their dogs to hunt larger game, for fresh meat to roast over the campfires.

Later she writes about the grandeur of the vast countryside: the wide blue sky, rugged mountain ranges in the distance, a golden ball of sun setting among the peaks, and the color and beauty of prairie sunsets. The breathtaking beauties of nature untamed by people stirred her soul and made her feel small before God's great work of creation. Then came days of rain, hordes of mosquitoes, and buffalo flies. They tried to cook over smoky fires with wet firewood. Discouragement, sickness, and short tempers dogged their tracks. Yet a thread of hope and cheer was woven through her entries. Their faith in God sustained them, singing birds cheered them, and pretty wildflowers, such as shy wild violets, morning glories, blue phlox, and sweet williams, delighted them.

They reached a fertile river bottom, with black loam soil, lush grasses, groves of timber, and a sparkling river. It was their promised land. Soon the sound of axes rang out over the valley as they felled trees to build their cabins. Idella helped to chink mud in between the logs, to keep out howling blizzard winds.

After their cabin was finished, they were still busy. Using an outdoor oven, Idella baked ten loaves of bread from wheat cracklings her pa had ground. She and her mother made lye soap. They dipped strings into hot tallow to make candles. They made wild plum preserves, churned butter, and hoed the sweet corn patch.

They got honey from a hollow locust bee tree and picked several pails of wild grapes. The little girls liked to swing on the vines. She wrote that Pa was going to the nearest town, thirty miles away, to buy a sewing machine to surprise Ma for her birthday.

Well, back to the present. That's about

enough writing for tonight. I'll add more tomorrow when I have a chance.

January 20

Today Mrs. Worthington wanted to discuss her great-great-grandmother's experiences. She was reading her old journal while I was summarizing the plot last evening. Mrs. Worthington enjoyed the story of how her great-great-grandparents found each other, so here it is:

Mae, Idella's older sister, had a beau named Mose, who had staked a claim on a neighboring homestead. But a claim jumper stole it from him. So in the spring, Mose headed west to find another fertile river bottom and build a cabin for his bride. He planned to return for his wedding in the fall. But he didn't show up. Poor Mae had to postpone the wedding.

A hard winter followed, with blizzards howling around their cabin as they huddled close to the fireplace to keep warm. Mae's sadness affected them all, and their spirits were low.

They set up the hickory-wood quilt frame and made more washed wool comforters, to keep the little shavers warm. Every night they heard wolves howling in the distance; sometimes they even came close to the cabin and barn, their hunger making them reckless and bold.

One night they were sitting around the big plank table, with yet another blizzard howling outside. Her dad and the older ones were dipping candles. Her mother was teaching the younger ones their three Rs, readin', 'ritin', and 'rithmetic. Then their dog began to bark ferociously. Visitors were rare, and they thought a wolf pack was about to eat the dog.

Then they heard a knock on the door and opened it to let in their next nearest neighbor, Joe Davis, from two miles away. His wife was in a bad way. He had come through the storm on the bobsled to fetch Idella's mother.

The next morning, Idella wrote, they all felt so sorry for him when they heard that both his young wife and newborn son had died. The ground was frozen too hard for a burial. They laid the mother in a coffin, with the baby in her arms, and packed the coffin into a snowbank till the spring thaw.

What hardships those brave pioneers had to face on the frontier! She wrote that she prayed daily for Joe Davis, that God would give him strength and courage to bear his double dose of sorrow.

Another year passed, with still no word about Mae's betrothed, Mose. So they sadly gave him up as dead in the dangerous wilderness. (I heard that pioneers had an average life span of about thirty-seven years.)

When young widower Joe asked for Mae's hand in marriage, she accepted, though her heart didn't seem to be in it, Idella reported. They prepared for a wedding in the cabin and summoned a circuit rider. Yet there was an undercurrent of sadness; Mae still longed for Mose.

Idella said, "Tomorrow is Mae's wedding day, and she acts like she's going to a funeral. I feel so sorry for Joe Davis, I could shake her. She should have refused him or at least act happy, for his sake."

They had invited everyone from miles around. The chickens were butchered, the potatoes peeled, the dried beans soaking, and the dried apple pies and cakes baked. In the morning, the guests arrived. The preacher began his sermon when they heard a clattering of hooves. A rider approached on a galloping horse. It was Mose, back to claim his bride, just in the nick of time!

He had been badly injured and had taken a long time to heal. Mose had sent a message but it had never reached them. When Mae called off the wedding, Idella felt so sorry for Joe that *she* offered to become his bride! A week later, before the traveling preacher left, they had a double wedding — Mae and Mose, and Idella and Joe!

I wish Idella would've written more about her feelings just then. I can't imagine what that would've been like. Just a few years later, her rich bachelor uncle willed his estate to her, his favorite niece, and they moved back east, to this old house.

Ya, well, it's time for bed. Maybe I can write the rest tomorrow night. I'll just add this much yet: in one of Idella's last entries, she wrote that they were never sorry for their hasty decision. They had a happy and peaceable marriage, loved each other deeply, and raised a fine family. They were Quakers who helped many mistreated slaves to gain freedom and were kind to others, too.

January 24

Last week Mrs. Worthington had an attack of bronchitis, and they called in a real nurse to care for her. So I was able to finish copying Idella's journal. Now it's Monday night. Tomorrow Grant is coming, so tonight is my last chance to have the journal, to scan it for anything I want to put into my diary.

I wasn't at the singing last night, so I got to bed early. Sadie and I had a long sisterly chat, though, and more and more I realize what a jewel of a sister she is. I wish I could be like her.

Now more about Idella. She tells of those first days as Mrs. Davis, of their cabin home, and of her darling little stepson, Jared. One winter day when Jared was two, Joe went to town for provisions. A northeaster blew up, and he couldn't make it home for the night. Jared was sick. A high wind was driving the snow. Idella was distracted in caring for the little boy and waited too long to add wood to the fire. The fire died out, and the cabin grew cold.

She knew she could not go through the storm to fetch live coals from the neighbors. Toward morning, Jared became croupy and tight. She had no experience with treating croup, but she remembered hearing that steam is good for loosening it. But alas, she had no fire for heating water. The little boy became worse. At daybreak he "passed on to be with the angels."

For a while, her remorse and guilt knew no bounds. Even though her husband was kind and understanding, it took a long time for her feelings to heal and for her to forgive herself. Not till they were back in the East and living in their new mansion, this very house, did they have another child, a daughter, Mrs. Worthington's great-grandmother.

Wouldn't it be interesting to travel back into that period and see this house and the whole countryside as it looked then? I would want to stop in at this big mansion to visit Idella and her husband and see the baby girl. She writes quite a bit about visitors they had in their secret room after they became active in operating a station of the Underground Railroad.

"Last night a family was brought in, hidden in a wagonload of hay. We gave them breakfast in our kitchen. The woman was looking scared, protecting her little boy, Clark, and eager to get back into hiding."

I'll have to ask our Clark if that was his great-grandfather. Clark once told me that when the war was over and the slaves were free, his great-great-grandfather brought his family back to this area and for years worked for Joe Davis (as hired help).

Around that time, Joe Davis became a Quaker, too, influenced by Idella — though some earlier entries hinted that maybe he would lead her away from being Quaker.

Time to rest, for I don't feel well. I have a steady, throbbing pain in my side, something I've endured, in a mild form, all day. I tried to ignore it, hoping it wouldn't get worse and that it wasn't appendicitis. But tonight it is worse. I hope I'll be able to sleep.

Maybe I can find something comforting to glean yet from *Gold Dust*.

Golden Gem for Today
Oh! Welcome the friendly voice that speaks to me
of hope, even in the midst of trouble.
I will receive with thanks the devotion and care that is kindly pressed upon me.
I will ask God to bless my kind friends and tell them: "All you have done for mine, I will repay you a hundredfold."

January 27

Here I am, back at home in our big cozy farm kitchen, sitting on a rocker with a quilt wrapped around me. Mamm and Sadie have my embroidered quilt in the frame, and they won't let me put even one stitch into it. On Monday night the pain became worse and worse instead of better, and I spent a sleepless night. By morning I was ready to see a doctor.

I ended up in the hospital, where I stayed for two days. Thinking it was appendicitis, they performed surgery. They discovered that the appendix wasn't even inflamed. But since they had gone to all that trouble, they took it out anyway! Oh, well, at least I'll not have to fear I'll get it at some later time! They said a gastrointestinal infection caused the pain and nausea.

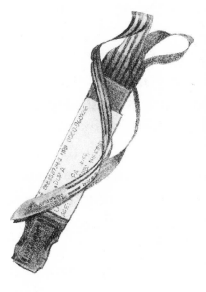

I've already received a few get-well cards in the mail, including one from Mrs. Worthington. I keep thinking of her and wondering how she's making out. I guess I missed the homecoming of her son, Grant. I suppose she'll have him to talk to now and won't miss me much.

January 28

It's good to be home and feeling better. As the quilting is done around the edges, we roll the quilt around the supporting sticks, and the frame takes less space. I enjoy helping to put stitches into the center now.

Sadie has left for her "baby nurse" job, and I really miss our sisterly chats. We're having more snow these days, but not in blizzard form. Big flakes of snow float lazily down most all day, not piling up much, but putting a clean layer of pure white on top of grungy old snow. Every night temperatures dip into single digits.

Barbianne was over this afternoon to help quilt. She began talking about when their first baby was stillborn and how devastated they felt when they feared they'd never be able to have any children. Now they have James and Joanna, and I don't believe they'll ever take them for granted. Joanna is such a sweet and demure little girl, and James has such a friendly smile.

Then tonight Priscilla brought Grandma Annie over, and the stretched-out part of the quilt became even smaller. Miriam Joy can quilt like a *Grossmammi*. Altogether, it was a most enjoyable evening. Now after taking the time to copy an inspirational verse, I'll write a long letter to Matthew.

Golden Gem for Today
*Lord, let each day seem wasted if it
passes without you making me into
a consoling angel,
helping me speak caring words,
or letting me be the cause of someone,
even a child, blessing your name.*

January 29

I'm back at the Worthingtons' Winslow Manor. I just missed Grant by a few hours. Early this morning, he left for a sunnier, warmer clime.

Once more the whole household is in a dither, preparing Mrs. Worthington for a long journey to visit a dear friend of hers for a week and to make a stop at Gloria Graham's house. She's not taking any of her maids along, saying there are plenty of maids in her friend's house. Instead, she asked me to accompany her!

I am quite excited about the trip, for I'm sure we won't be traveling in a crowded van, but in comfort and style. We'll see parts of the world I'd otherwise never get to see, and in the middle of winter, too. I suppose Mrs. Worthington feels that because of her prestige and importance, the weather will cooperate and the roads will automatically clear for her — the snow will melt before her as she goes (smiles).

No time to do much writing today. Besides tending to Mrs. Worthington, I must get my clothes ready and my bags packed. It will be a simple matter, though, compared to the amount of clothes in suit-cases that she's having her maids pack for her. I've looked into her closets, and she must have at least a hundred dresses and fifty pairs of shoes, along with oodles of accessories. I'm glad I'm not burdened with so many possessions.

Time to scoot.

January 31

I'm ashamed now, of my flippant comments about Mrs. Worthington, the weather, and the roads. She was intending to go by plane. When I found it out, I had to tell her I won't be going along after all, because our *Ordnung* (church rules) allow that only for an emergency. She then immediately canceled her plans. Now we're going in her son's motor home.

There's another surprise. When she told me she's going to visit her friend at Millwyck Manor and stop at Gloria Graham's house, I assumed that Millwyck Manor was in Arizona, too. But it's not, for Gloria has recently moved. She lives about a hundred miles south of where Matthew is working in California, so I'll be able to visit him there! I am quite excited and delighted about that!

Tomorrow we leave, with Clark driving the motor home. The weather has turned somewhat milder, and the roads, at least around here, are clear. I hope we won't run into snowstorms or get stranded anywhere, and I hope I won't be too excited to sleep.

February 2

Our prayers are being answered: the roads remain in good shape as we journey westward toward St. Louis, Missouri, the Gateway to the West. Clark is a careful driver, and Mrs. Worthington is resting comfortably.

I can't help but think that this way of traveling to the West is so much more comfortable than bumping along in a covered wagon, like the early pioneers. Would Idella have liked to ride in a motor home, with beds handy, and kitchen and bath provided? We are lounging in luxury but mostly cut off from nature, not able to hear the birds, see many roadside flowers, or feel the wind or rain in our faces as we speed along.

The closer we get to our destination, the more my thoughts travel to seeing Matthew. Mrs. Worthington has been asking questions about our courtship standards and our wedding plans.

She asked, "Is it true that you believe the husband should be the head of the wife, and that she must be submissive to him at all times, giving up her will to his?"

Somehow, when she puts it that way, it doesn't sound right, and it didn't sound as if she approved of it, either. She pressed me even further: "Are you sure this is what you want? Women have the right to make their own decisions as well as the men. After all, staying single is just as noble and worthy a calling as marriage."

She read me a few verses from the apostle Paul, saying that the unmarried woman cares for the things of the Lord, that she may be holy in both body and spirit. But the married woman cares for the things of the world, how she may please her husband. Paul says that the unmarried woman has more time to care for the things of the Lord, while the married woman is more distracted by doing things for her husband.

Then Mrs. Worthington fell asleep. When she woke up, she apologized for trying to discourage me. She said, "Everyone must follow the Lord's leading. God's grace will be sufficient on whatever path God's will lies. Each of us must submit to God's will, whatever that may be."

Ya, well, I'm not discouraged. She hasn't met Matthew yet. When she does, she will get over the notion that he will be a dictator.

I could have told her that when the husband does his part in treating his wife with love and kindness, her part of being submissive will be easy. I suppose her theory that a wife need not be submissive to her husband is one of the reasons why there are so many divorces among the *Englischers* (non-Amish).

I have my *Gold Dust* along, and I think I'll copy a verse yet.

Golden Gem for Today
If it's God's will to send trials,
be patient and humble.

*Weep if your heart is sore, but love always,
and wait.
The trial will pass away,
but God will remain yours forever.*

February 7

Here we are at Gloria Graham's house. It's hard to believe how unseasonably mild and balmy the weather is here in California, just north of San Francisco. No wonder she chose this spot. From her hilltop bungalow, there's a magnificent view of the countryside and the Pacific Ocean.

On her back terrace there's a concrete pool with lots of pink, white, yellow, and lavender water lilies floating on top. Water is bubbling out of fountains that look like statues. There are water hyacinths and bright orange goldfish, and koi (a carp) darting and swimming here and there among the underwater foliage.

Gloria is as effusive and gushing as ever. She and Mrs. Worthington, being two of a kind, hit it off well. She keeps telling Mrs. Worthington how blessed she is to have me for a traveling companion. But really, I'm the one blessed to be able to go along to visit Matthew.

She has a pet poodle, and how she does

pamper and spoil that little dog! I remember how we used to think that Gloria was so silly and childish, the way she used to treat her cat like a queen. But now I think that everyone who lives alone ought to have the love and devotion of a pet, one who loyally accepts you and loves you through thick and thin. I've heard that it's good for your emotional health to have a pet that depends on you and needs you to care for it.

We didn't see anything of her husband, George, and I didn't want to ask. Maybe he was away on a trip. We did see some men's clothes in the hall closet.

Tonight I have a lovely room to sleep in, with lacy curtains, soft plush rugs, and a beautiful bedspread. There's even a television set here, but I wouldn't know how to turn it on even if I wanted to. I probably wouldn't be able to sleep if I'd watch the kind of stuff they say is on television nowadays.

February 8

We spent the forenoon exploring Golden Gate Gardens, with its acres and acres of beautifully landscaped lawns and gardens. I would love to see it in the spring when all the bulbs are blooming, or in June when the roses are at their finest. The acres of greenhouses are the main attraction at this time of year, filled with exotic plants and flowers of exquisite sweetness.

We saw streams and fountains, waterfalls and pools, beautiful displays and arrangements, delights beyond description. Mrs. Worthington remarked, "It's heavenly, out of this world."

They even had a simulated thunderstorm: all became dark, while thunder crashed, lightning flashed, and raindrops began to fall. Before the daylight came back, a display of spectacular illuminated fountains came on, and the dazzling, glimmering color was awesome.

It would've been even more awesome, though, if it had been a natural display, like the northern lights, instead of man-made. The guide told us that when a tree or large shrub dies, they replace it with a full-grown one that has to be brought in by helicopter. I wish Matthew could've been along to see all this.

February 9, Morning

Yesterday we arrived at Millwyck Manor, even more impressive than Winslow Manor because everything is new and modern. It must have cost a million dollars to build. Mrs. Millwyck (as I call her) is kind and gracious. But I'm feeling quite lost in this place of modern finery and luxury, for Mrs. Worthington isn't here. If it weren't for Clark, I'd feel totally abandoned.

Let me explain. In the middle of the night, a maid awoke me and summoned me to Mrs. Worthington's bedside. Mrs. Millwyck was there, holding her hand, and an ambulance was on its way. Mrs. Worthington is allergic to some things, and apparently something in her room had triggered an attack.

I felt so sorry for her, but there wasn't much I could do. Mrs. Millwyck insisted on going along to the hospital in the ambulance.

This morning Mrs. Millwyck called home to say that Mrs. Worthington is stabilized and out of danger, but they've found a heart murmur. She'll have to stay for a few days till they find the right medication for her. They transferred her to another hospital better able to deal with her condition, one sixty miles from here.

Clark made some inquiries, and discovered that the hospital she's in is actually closer to Matthew's workplace than it is to

Millwyck Manor. So we'll be heading for the hospital shortly. If Mrs. Worthington doesn't need me to stay with her, we'll visit for several hours, then head on out to Kendleton's Horse and Brahma Farm in northern California.

I'm afraid Matthew will be so surprised he will be stunned speechless. I know I would be. He does not know we are coming. I can hardly wait to see the expression on his face!

February 9, Evening

Now we're on our way to Matthew's place, and I'm getting more and more excited about surprising him! We found Mrs. Worthington in good spirits and had a nice visit with her.

Mrs. Worthington knows how excited I am about visiting Matthew, so she insisted I don't have to stay with her. Mrs. Millwyck, her dear and longtime friend, is staying with her all the time she's in the hospital, so I felt easy about leaving her.

Clark has been talkative while he drives, and I appreciate it, for it seems to have a calming effect on me. The closer we get to our destination, the more fidgety I get. I think I should prick myself with my cape pin to see if all this is for real or whether I'll wake up from a dream.

February 10

Last evening my first impression of the farm was of its splendid surrounding scenery as we drove under the big arched sign posted over the entrance drive. It welcomed us to KENDLETON'S HORSE AND BRAHMA FARM. The sun was just setting in a maze of gold, sending its last bright rays over the countryside.

In the field west of the farm is a huge pond with an encircling road, on which the horses are exercised. The field to the east is dotted with cattle.

As we drove up to the buildings, a young man came driving up from the pond road on a sulky, a two-wheeled training cart, drawn by an Appaloosa horse. The minute I saw him, even though it was too far away to see his features, I knew it was Matthew. When he recognized me, the look on his face was priceless!

Matthew gave me a grand welcome. Later he said, "I thought I must be dreaming." He was delighted to see me, and I was so happy to see him.

We had a wonderful evening. He showed me all through the horse barns and explained his work. It's a little too early for the spring crop of colts, but the yearlings are interesting, too, and the brood mares and stallions. The cattle are in his care now, too, and I followed him around and helped wherever I could, feeding the weaned calves and colts.

Matthew was extra busy because Mr. Kendleton was slightly injured yesterday by one of his prize Brahma bulls. It was late when we finished the chores.

Then we took a stroll out a country lane yet. There was so much to talk about, and so much catching up to do. A silvery moon was coming up over the treetops, just like back home. It was a perfect evening in every way!

I'm at the Kendleton house now, half a mile up the road from the farm. I spent the night here, which suited Mrs. Kendleton well, for otherwise she would've been alone. This afternoon when she visits her husband at the hospital, I'll go along to visit Mrs. Worthington since they're in the same hospital.

Matthew lives with the tenant farmer family, and I plan to spend time there again today, helping out wherever I can.

With Mr. Kendleton gone, they are short-handed. Clark has gone back to the city and has taken a hotel room close to the hospital until Mrs. Worthington is released.

It's early morning now, too early to disturb Mrs. Kendleton. She's a *gutmehnich* (kindhearted) person, saying, "We depend on Matthew's help so much. He's such a good and dependable worker. We don't see how we'll be able to do without his help when he leaves."

She even offered to find us a house in the area to rent, if we would consider coming here to live after we're married. Then Matthew could keep his job, with a raise thrown in besides.

I told her I'll have to talk it over with Matthew. But I'm sure her proposal will be out of the question. We will want our family to be among our own people so it will be easier for us to follow our way of life.

February 12

Yesterday and today have been quite busy. All morning I was helping the tenant farmer's wife, and I hardly saw anything of Matthew until lunchtime. Then I spent the afternoon with Mrs. Worthington at the hospital. In the evening Matthew and I took the time to walk down to the pond and talk.

He says, "I love my job here, but it's not good to be away from others of the same faith all week." He's looking forward to getting back to our people. Matthew compared it to separating a hot coal from the rest of the fire. "That isolated coal will soon burn out. If it stays with the rest of the coals, it will continue to glow."

I've felt somewhat the same way while working for Mrs. Worthington. It's not good for me to be away from our people all week, even though I attend church every other Sunday, as usual. I can understand why Mamm was reluctant to let me go.

Matthew, too, spends his weekends with distant relatives in Reedsville whenever he can. He and I will travel there on Saturday evening and attend church there on Sunday. I look forward to that, for it seems so long since we've been with others of like precious faith.

At the hospital, I found Mrs. Worthington still in good spirits. They have her on medication that stabilizes her heartbeat, and the doctors plan to release her in a few days. I peeked in on Mr. Kendleton, too, and he appeared to be a fine, respectable man. Matthew says he is a fair and reasonable employer.

Down by the pond, Matthew and I sat on a rustic old bench by the shore and watched the yearlings frolicking in their corral, glad to be let out for their evening run. We had so much catching up to do, talking and planning, that the evening sped by as if on wings. Before we knew it, the moon was overhead and the night was half over.

He walked with me up to Mrs. Kendleton's house, and then we now sat awhile yet on the porch swing. Courtship by mail has lost every bit of its luster. Now it seems like an awfully long time till the lilacs blossom.

February 14, Valentine's Day

Clark drove out here on Saturday evening and took Matthew and me over to Reedsville. We passed the farm where Matthew used to work. That night Clark slept in the motor home, and Matthew stayed with a friend of his. The Steurys took me in since they have a daughter just my age.

They dress a bit differently from our

way. Their *Kapps* (caps) are not quite the same as ours, though still made of organdy, and their capes are made with their own design.

For the Sunday meeting yesterday, I rode with the Steurys in their carriage to another farmhouse, and it was just like our church services at home. The only difference was that they used a slightly different tune for the same songs we sing, and maybe sang slower.

Rhoda Steury is an outgoing girl, and I felt at home with this friendly family right away. In the evening Matthew borrowed a horse and buggy, and we drove to the singing together. It was interesting to be there. Rhoda made sure that I wasn't made to feel like an outsider. The singing part of the evening was exceptionally beautiful; they have a few really talented singers there.

We took our time driving back to Steurys' place. There was so much to discuss, and our time together is short. Our borrowed horse didn't have much pep, so Matthew decided that we could save a few miles by taking a shortcut through a field lane between two farms.

All went as planned until two chunky workhorses, who had somehow gotten out of their stable, came running up alongside, scaring our trusty old steed into a gallop. We had a wild ride, but Matthew had our horse calmed down by the time we reached the road.

At Steurys' house, a horse with a trottin' buggy was tied at the railing. The parlor was already occupied by Rhoda and her chap, so we had our date in the kitchen, by the light of a kerosene lamp. By and by, Rhoda and her Ephraim joined us there. Rhoda made hot chocolate and brought out from the pantry *Schnitzboi* (snitz pie, made of sliced, dried fruit). Thus another evening flew by as if on wings. All too soon it was time for Matthew to leave, another evening of our too-short visit gone.

Clark drove out this morning and took us back to the Kendletons' farm. Mr. Kendleton was released on Saturday and was strolling around outside, feeling much better. I helped to feed the cattle and horses this morning, then helped to do baking in the kitchen.

Right after lunch Matthew led me behind a lilac bush, with buds in winter dormancy, waiting to swell and blossom come spring. He said he had made something special for me. It was a beautiful red valentine, saying,

Love is patient.
Love is kind.
I am yours,
but
Are you mine?

I gave him a warm thank-you and whispered, "Yes, I'm your valentine." What a *Liebschdi* (sweetheart) my Matthew is!

This afternoon Clark and I visited Mrs. Worthington. We found her happy to announce that she will be released tomorrow, ready to head back to Millwyck Manor. This visit sure has turned out differently from what she had planned. At least she did get to visit with Mrs. Millwyck, even though it was in the hospital.

We arrived at home late Saturday evening, and I spent yesterday (Sunday) at home with Mamm and Daed. It was so good to be home. All the clan was there for supper (Henry's, Rudy's, Grandpa Dave's) to hear about my trip. They all seemed so dear and precious. But it just didn't seem right that Matthew couldn't be there. I comforted myself with the thought that it's less than three months until lilac blossom time.

After they left, I had a talk with Mamm. She encouraged me to accept my coming marriage as God's purpose for me and to see what a blessing lies in it. It was good to have Mamm confirming what I was already feeling. Sadie wanted to know every detail of our trip and visit, so after we were in bed, we chatted long into the night. She is the kind who delights and rejoices in the happiness of others and hasn't a jealous bone in her.

Now I'm back again at my job at Winslow Manor. I contented myself with writing a long letter to Matthew tonight. I took it downstairs and gave it to Clark to put in the mail tomorrow morning. He gave me the news that Grant arrived home several hours ago, just back from the tropics. Maybe this time I'll get to visit with him. I think it would be interesting to see him again, now that I know more about him and know that Clark was like a dad to him.

I went back in to see Mrs. Worthington after she was settled comfortably in bed. She told me that Grant is reading Idella McNeil's journal and is quite attracted to it, recognizing his ancestors and heritage. She even mentioned something again about me copying it for her future grandchildren and having me read it to her.

I'm glad she's better again. As she sat up in her big four-poster bed, her cheeks were pink and her lips bright red. I suppose she used a little rouge to appear bright and well to her son, Grant, for she's been quite tired since we're back. I think the trip home was a bit much for her, so soon after her hospital stay.

I feel a little guilty for being the reason she decided not to travel by plane, as she had planned. That would've been much faster and easier for her. I think she was a little hurt, too, that Grant didn't spend his evening visiting with her, instead of reading the old journal. She told me she's feeling downhearted and dreads the day that I must leave her. I resolved to try to cheer her up, but I wasn't all that successful.

Afterward, I came up to my room to read a chapter out of my Bible, as I do every evening, and to write in my journal. I'll take the time to copy something out of *Gold Dust* again tonight, too, since I've been neglecting it the last while.

Golden Gem for Today

People with small virtue
need the praise of others to sustain them,
just as infants need encouragement to
walk or stand alone.
But people of true virtue go quietly through
the world, scattering good around
and performing noble deeds,
without knowing that the doing is heroic.

February 23

I don't often get a letter in the mail here at Winslow Manor, but today I did, and my heart skipped a few beats when I saw who it was from. Mamm forwarded it to me. I guess she knew I'd be anxious to receive it now rather than wait for the weekend. She wanted to add a letter of her own, too, maybe thinking I needed some cheering up myself.

The letter was from Enos and Betty Miller of Minnesota. They're expecting a baby in March, probably about a month from now, and the girl they had lined up to help them can't do it for some reason. So they're out on a limb and need me.

I know that girls out there who are available to work as a *Maad* (hired girl) are scarce, since the community has mostly young families with small children. I really want to go, and I'll write them a reply tonight yet, telling them that I'll come. They even offered to pay my transportation and to line up a reserved seat in a vanload, whenever there's a chance.

Now I must go downstairs and tell Mrs. Worthington. I think she'll be glad to hear that I have a job lined up. Her former maid sent word today that she's regained her health and will be back to her job shortly. It *schpeids* me (makes me sorry) to leave Mrs. Worthington because I've grown quite fond of her in the weeks I've been here. She's a dear old lady with a likable personality, so *gutmehnich* (kind-hearted).

I haven't seen anything of Grant since he's home, and I hope I'll get the chance before I leave on Friday for the weekend.

On Monday morning, I was all ready and waiting for Clark to come and pick me up at home and take me back to my job for another week. I was wishing, as I always do these days, that it were May instead of a dreary, foggy February morning. I wanted the big old lilac bush in the backyard to burst into bloom instead of just starting to push tiny buds.

When Clark came driving in the lane, he didn't wait for me to come out. He came walking to the house. Through the window I noticed with a pang how old and stooped and careworn he looked. My heart went out to him, knowing he must be the bearer of bad news. He has also been a dear friend to me.

Nearly every morning while I was there, I spent some time sitting in his basement shop and working on my quilt patches while he worked on his carving projects. I got to know him quite well and found him to be a sincere and good-hearted Christian, as trustworthy as anyone I know. My heart ached for him; I was sure he was going to tell me that Mrs. Worthington had gotten terribly sick and was in the hospital or had even died.

But it wasn't that. Instead, he told me that Winslow Manor burned down last night! Everyone got out safely and without injury, but they couldn't save the house. Clark explained how the fire started.

Grant was stretched out on a sofa in the library, reading Idella McNeil's old journal and smoking cigarettes. He flicked some ashes into what he thought was an ashtray. If he had looked properly, he would have seen that it was a small box with a few facial tissues in the bottom. He left for an evening of partying. Shortly afterward, the fire sprang up and ignited newspapers and books nearby on the table, and then eventually the whole room burst into flames.

Mrs. Worthington was in bed, the maids were all in another wing of the house, and Clark was in his basement workshop, also under another wing of the house. The blaze was rather far advanced by the time the smoke and crackling sounds reached Clark. By the time he had everyone safely out, the wind had swept the flames to the rest of the mansion. When the firefighters arrived, it was beyond saving.

We sure have a lot to be thankful for that everyone got out safely! Mrs. Worthington got a heart spell and was taken to the doctor, but he assured her that it was only nervous palpitations. Clark took her and her maids to a friend's home in the city.

I invited Clark to come and stay with us, but he said he didn't think it would be necessary. Other arrangements are being made. I suppose there is no lack of funds for whatever they decide to do. But no amount of money can replace Idella McNeil's priceless old journal.

March 3

There was a faint trace of a feel of spring in the air tonight as I walked home from Henry and Priscilla's place. I heard a robin bravely singing in spite of the brisk wind and the dark clouds gathering in the evening sky. Next month will be April with its warm breezes and spring flowers, and then May and lilac blossom time!

Dear Diary, you are probably weary of this refrain, but it's the song of my heart. Why does time insist on crawling so slowly these days?

Priscilla is wholeheartedly into caring for prison babies again, and I enjoyed helping out today and yesterday. Those little dark-skinned tykes she has now are so cute and adorable. I've secretly been thinking that someday maybe I could help to care for foster babies, too, when our own family of boys and girls are all grown up and have left the nest. (I hope to have at least a dozen!) But counting chicks before they're hatched is not proper or dignified. I must deal with the here and now and quit building castles in the air.

I haven't heard anything from Clark or Mrs. Worthington now since Monday morning, and I'm wondering how they're making out. I'll take the time yet to copy an inspirational verse from *Gold Dust*.

Golden Gem for Today
The inner life is an abiding sense
of God's presence,
a constant union with God.
We learn to look upon the heart as the temple
where God dwells, and we act, think, speak,
and fulfill all our duties as in God's presence.

March 4

I had a surprise today when Clark took me to visit Mrs. Worthington at the Harmony Acres Nursing Home. With a chuckle, he said, "She's been asking for you and gave me no peace until I went for you." Her new abode is a grand and elaborate place, where I imagine only the rich and elite lodge.

Clark is also staying in a small apartment at the place. He has access to the workshop there, which will likely be his lifeline, now that everything else is gone.

Mrs. Worthington has a suite of rooms even more elegantly furnished than Winslow Manor had been. She seems to be happy there, pleased that she can have her own personal maid. At this point, she does not plan to rebuild and says Grant can do that if he wishes, since he will inherit everything.

I'm glad I was able to visit her. I think I can quit feeling sorry for her now, for she's well taken care of. She's happy that I have another job lined up and wants me to write to her regularly.

When Clark brought me home, he presented me with a big, carefully wrapped package. He told me that it's a parting gift for me, and that I wasn't to open it until I was in the house. How like him, not wanting to be the object of praise or thanks. I must be sure to send him a thank-you note.

In the package was the beautiful, intricately-carved stagecoach and horses I had so admired on the shelf in his workshop! Luckily, he had loaned it to a friend to use as a model in a painting, and so it escaped the fire and was preserved. What a nice remembrance I'll have of Clark, in the years to come, one that I'll always cherish.

March 6

I hadn't received a letter from Matthew for a while and was beginning to be worried, wondering why he hadn't written his usual weekly letter. At last, today it came, calming my heart and soothing my worries. He wrote that he was quite sick for a week, miserable and feverish with swollen cheeks. I guessed it right away — the mumps! I wonder how he ever escaped having them when he was a child — or did he have them twice?

Matthew wrote that he must have picked up the mumps from the tenant farmer's little boy, who was not nearly as sick as Matthew became. The doctor said mumps

usually affects adults more severely than children.

Whew! I'm so glad to hear that my *Liebschdi* (sweetheart) is well again. I must write to him now to tell him about my planned job with Enos Millers, and to send him my new address. But first I'll glean something from *Gold Dust*. I'm glad I hadn't left it at Winslow Manor to perish in the fire. It must be a rare book by now and could hardly be replaced.

Golden Gem for Today
Prayer is the key to all celestial treasures.
Through prayer, we penetrate into
the midst of all
the joy, strength, mercy, and goodness divine.
We receive our well-being from all around us,
as the sponge plunged into the ocean imbibes
without effort the surrounding water.
Thereby joy, strength, mercy, and
goodness become our own.

After a long, tiresome journey by van, this finds me at the Enos and Betty Miller home. It seems like old times, but there is a difference. I remember when I came here the first time to help out when Betty was sick, how forlorn I felt. Everywhere I turned, there was work staring me in the face: stacks of dirty dishes on the counter, piles of laundry to be done, the kitchen needing cleaning, and the children ailing.

By the end of the first day, my spirits were drooping. I was afraid it would be an awful grind, nothing but hurry, hurry, hurry, and I'd never get caught up, no matter how much I tried.

Today when I arrived, however, the kitchen was spotless. All the work seemed to be done on schedule. The preschoolers were quietly playing with their building block set, and there was a row of freshly baked loaves of bread on the counter.

I am really not needed here yet, but I had to come when the vanload did. When I offered to do some spring housecleaning for Betty, she told me it's all finished. So she put me to mending pants instead. With such a row of active boys, I suppose someone must constantly keep after such a job. When that was finished, I made a dozen shoofly and apple schnitz pies, plus several double portions of molasses cookies.

Tonight, as I think back to the other time I worked here, I'm ashamed of how I misjudged this family in their time of trial, with Betty not well and in and out of the hospital. I was younger and under stress myself.

Yet my face blushes with shame when I think of how standoffish and uncommunicative I was toward Enos. Poor man, I wonder how he could put up with me. I blamed him for being like a "great silent bear" around the house, and I was actually describing myself! How many times did Enos try to strike up a friendly conversation that I squelched!

Never once did I write in my diary about the times he got the children ready for bed and told them their bedtime Bible stories, or the times he gave the little ones their baths. I didn't mention the times he helped me finish getting a meal on the table when I was late with it. He was willing to lend a hand in many other ways.

Oh yes, I could justify myself, saying I was overwhelmed with the work and responsibilities there. But still I'm glad I have the chance to show them I'm sorry and want to do better. I think I've done some growing up myself since I was first here — at least I hope so.

I was amazed at the change in Betty, too. What a difference between poor health and good health! The last time I was here, she was still thin and pale, but now she's plump (of course) and rosy-cheeked, the picture of health.

Time for bed, if I don't want to over-sleep tomorrow morning. I need to mesh into the family routine.

March 20

Now my "baby nurse" job starts for real. Early this morning, before the children were awake, I heard a tiny baby crying downstairs in the corner bedroom. A few minutes later I heard the midwife's car starting up and driving out the lane.

Soon Enos called me, and I had the happy task of weighing and dressing the fat little bundle: a chubby nine-pound, twelve-ounce boy named Alpheus. The midwife had to rush on to another place or she would have done that fun part herself.

This is the Millers' tenth child. Never-theless, Betty said, "The tenth one is just

How the little girls love to hold and rock the new little bundle. Sometimes there are spats, too, when they can't agree on whose turn it is. He is *braav* (good) and sleeps on, oblivious to how he is being passed around. When it's my turn, I marvel at how perfectly formed he is, how adorably sweet and precious. His little hands curl around my fingers, his eyes are the bluest of blue, and he has a cleft in his chin that quivers when he cries. Baby Alpheus has even smiled already in his sleep.

Betty asked me if I'd be willing to keep working here at least till May first. The doctor has told her she needs to stay off her feet for a few weeks and take some prescribed medicine because she has phlebitis in one leg. Even after she is up, she will need my help for a while.

Of course, I said I would stay. That's getting close to lilac blossom time, when Matthew comes back! I hope another job will turn up for me then, so I can stay here in this community until it's time for me to go back home to Pennsylvania and get ready for our wedding.

I'm counting the months now. Soon it will be weeks, then only days. Time flies

as rare and precious a gift from God as the first one was. The miracle of birth is just as awesome."

Holding and cuddling such a sweet little bundle is such an exquisite experience that it brought tears to my eyes. A gift from God! What would it be like for me to be holding my own little angelic bundle in my arms?

When the children came downstairs and heard the news, they sure were a happy and excited bunch! I admire the wisdom of Enos and Betty in choosing a name first thing. If they had given the children a chance, each of them would have proposed a different name.

Golden Gem for Today
A well-spent day is a source of pleasure.
The secret of much goodness and
happiness is being
constantly employed yet never asking,
"What shall I do?" Begin then,
by being prompt, acting decisively,
and persevering. If interrupted,
be amiable
and return to work unruffled.
Finish it carefully.
These are signs of a virtuous soul.

It should not be hard for me to practice

some of these virtues here at the Millers'. I'll certainly do my best, with God's help.

March 21

Baby Alpheus is doing well and growing as he should. He apparently thrives on being passed around from child to child, as they beg for turns in holding him.

Today is the first day of spring, and it feels a bit like it, too. At least the snow is melting and red-winged blackbirds are back. I think the pussy willows will soon be blooming. We had our first meal of dandelion greens for supper, and 'twas delicious, made with a bit of chopped bacon and hard-boiled eggs, with a dab of vinegar added.

There's a mild south wind blowing tonight, and spring peepers (small frogs) are singing. Tonight, after dumping out the dishwater, I stayed in the yard for a while, watching the majestic, copper-colored moon rise over the treetops. I wondered whether Matthew saw it, too. In just a few more months, the lilacs will be blooming, and he will be back. Then our courtship by mail will be a thing of the past.

I'm really enjoying my job here at the Millers', and I'm becoming quite attached to this lovable family. The boys' good natured teasing and bantering keep interesting. The little girls' chatter amusing. Little Katie is just learning talk sentences, and her lisp is so Betty, already up enough to rest on recliner, does all the managing. I r now what a blessing such a big fam and how blessed Enos and Betty are.

I've had some heart-to-heart talks Betty. I hope someday I can be a wife like her. No wonder Enos loves her d as she loves him, with their mutual ness and unselfishness. I hope Ma and I can have a relationship ju blessed.

I think I'll copy something about out of *Gold Dust* yet, before I head for

Golden Gem for Today

*The core of true love is not tenderne
but strength, power to endure, purity
and self-giving.
It is a mistake if we seek to be belov
instead of focusing on loving.
Cowards fear to lose the other's love
A selfish heart desires love for itself,
a Christian heart delights in loving
and does not worry about
whether love will be returned.*

when you don't want it to and crawls when you wish it would fly.

April 1, First of April Jokes

These Miller children love to play April Fools' pranks on each other. Enos and Betty don't seem to mind, but they don't allow the children to say "April Fool." Instead, they say "First of April Joke." That's because it says in the Bible that it's wrong to call someone a fool.

This morning before breakfast, Betty told Enos Jr. to bring a crock of apple butter out of the pantry. He went, and from the pantry he suddenly yelled, "A mouse! A mouse in the apple butter!" Everyone jumped up from the table to see it, and then Enos emerged from the pantry, grinning mischievously, and said "First of April!"

This gave Uria ideas. When he went to the cellar for eggs, he came running up the steps yelling, "A skunk! A skunk!" Dad Enos wasn't tricked this time, but the others were, and the little girls screamed, until Uria triumphantly said, "First of April!"

Then this afternoon I had put a kettle of cornmeal mush on the back of the stove to simmer until suppertime. I was out on the porch, setting out pansies into a planter, when little Atlee came running out, yelling, "The mush is burning! The mush is burning!"

I jumped up so hastily that the planter overturned, spilling out the dirt. He was so delighted with being able to trick me that he could hardly stop giggling.

They're all so lovable, and I sure will miss them when I leave. I'm so glad I have this second chance to work here and to get to know the family better.

Age Twenty-One

Lilac Blossoms and Glory Bells

April 22

I just turned twenty-one on April 10. What will this year of my life bring me? Matthew, I hope! What will I bring to this year? Patience and dedication, I hope.

Time speeds by on work-laden wings, as it always does when one is busy and healthy and not unreasonably impatient for some future event. Enos cultivated the garden, and I planted five pounds of peas, with the children's help. With this growing family, it sure takes a lot of vegetables. If all goes well, by fall the can shelves will be loaded with the garden's bounties.

It's lawn-mowing time, too, and it sure helps to keep youngsters busy and out of mischief. One pushes the old reel mower, and another pulls a rope tied to the front (like a horse hitched to it) so that mowing goes easier.

I did the laundry this morning. As is fairly common, I had trouble starting the washing machine engine. I yanked and yanked on the starter cord, rested awhile, then yanked some more. Finally I gave up and trudged out to the barn to find Enos or the boys, but they were already out in the field.

From the back end of the barn, I heard a little boy shouting at the top of his lungs. I quickly ran to see what the trouble was. It was Atlee. He had climbed on top of a hay rack and fallen, and his pants had caught on a nail. There he was, hanging upside down and helpless, until I rescued him.

I took him in for Betty to doctor his bruises. The amazing part of it was that then I decided to try again to start the washing machine engine, and it sprang to life beautifully on the first try! Maybe it was providential that things happened this way, so I could rescue Atlee. No one would've heard him from the house.

May Day

The lilac buds are swelling, and Matthew should be home sometime this month! The Millers have asked me to stay another month. Enos is farming ten acres of a neighboring farm and will be putting it all in produce. Betty's phlebitis is better, but she still has to keep her leg elevated at times. So they will be glad for my help.

The weather has turned quite warm. Spring lambs are baaing and running with their mamas on the hillside. The children are excited about the new twin babies — in the barn, that is. Yesterday two tiny colts were born to their driving mare. Now they are hobbling around on unsteady legs by the side of their protective mother. They look exactly alike, with a star on the forehead and two partly white hind legs.

Tonight I took the little girls out to see the colts. When one of them whinnied a high baby whinny, he was immediately answered by well-wishing whinnies from all the other horses in the barn. It's probably a great event for them, too, having twin colts in the barn — a rare phenomenon.

Time for bed, but first I'll copy a bit out of *Gold Dust*.

Golden Gem for Today
How blessed, O Lord,
to depend only upon you.
I will pray fervently that I may
receive your presence, goodness, and love.
My heart shall be a sanctuary into which
nothing shall penetrate that could
be displeasing to you.

May 15

Matthew is home! I believe I feel about like those slaves that Clark was telling me about; when they crossed the border into Canada, they heard the glory bells ringing!

We had our date here in Betty's *Sitzschtubb* (sitting room), but we spent most of our time outdoors, walking and talking. We strolled out to the Millstream Orchards Farm, a half mile west of Enos's farmhouse, but still with land adjoining. Enos is renting ten acres from that farm.

On the property there's a quaint old mill, no longer used. Water in the millrace is flowing out from under the mill wheel and joining a small stream. There are several acres of old orchards, and the gnarled old apple trees in it are in bloom, giving the place an aura of incredible sweetness. It's also an excellent hideaway for lots of wildlife and birds.

There are three ponds, earlier used for irrigating, I suppose. Birds were singing everywhere. We turned into the gravel lane. A rusty old signpost held up a creaking sign that swayed in the breeze and announced MILLSTREAM ORCHARDS FARM. I don't think anyone lives there now, since it's looking unkempt.

As we explored the place, we saw lots of wildlife, such as bunnies, squirrels, and woodchucks, and birds of all kinds. We even saw two does run through the orchard and disappear into a spruce stand.

There is a possibility that this entire farm may come up for rent next year. We decided that if it does, we'll put our bid in for first chance at it. There's a lot of good farmland, besides the old orchards. The barn has enough cow stanchions in it for us to start dairying, although probably not up-to-date enough for shipping grade A milk.

The house is old but elegant looking. The porch trellises are overgrown with climbing roses. The roof has a cupola on top. There are even three lilac bushes in the front yard, the old-fashioned wild kind that are more fragrant than the modern ones. An old honeysuckle-covered stone wall stretches all around the front yard. They're late this year and not yet blooming, but we plan to go back again next Sunday evening.

I won't go into details about our date (I'll save that for my secret journal). Matthew and I have picked out our wedding date now: November 16, Lord willing. I'll head back to Mamm and Daed's in plenty of time to help get ready for the wedding. Matthew won't come until a week or two before the wedding.

Tonight I'm dreaming dreams and thinking deep thoughts, imagining what it would be like to live with Matthew at the Millstream Orchards Farm.

Tonight Betty sent me upstairs to get something for her out of her washstand drawer. Among some other keepsakes, I found a poem she had hand-copied. I slipped it into my pocket, meaning to ask her permission to copy it, too. But when I came downstairs, I forgot all about it. Oh, well, I guess I'll go ahead and copy it. She's already in bed now, and I'm sure she won't mind. Here it is:

A Bride's Prayer

Dear Father, now I come to you,
A humble, grateful bride;

132

Be ever near me through the years,
Oh, be my constant guide.

Help me, O God, to do your will,
Let nothing come between;
When cares and sorrows come to pass,
Lord, let me on you lean.

Dear Father, help me ever to be
A Christian wife and mother;
And may our home be filled with love,
O God, for one another.

Help me to overlook the things
That may bring clouds of sadness;
And in their stead, oh, help me spread
Kind thoughts of Christian gladness.

Give me an understanding heart,
Let wisdom be my guide;
These favors, loving Father, grant,
To me, a new-made bride.

In Jesus' name, Amen. (anon.)

I'm trying to imagine Betty as a young, sweet, rosy-cheeked bride, copying this poem, and praying for the grace to be a true companion for her new husband. She is still pretty, but her hair is streaked with gray, and her figure is dumpy. But I would say that her prayers have been answered for her marriage. I hope I can be as good as she is, and "spread kind thoughts of Christian gladness," as the poem says.

May 22

Last evening, Sunday, I was invited to Matthew's parents' place for supper. I believe they are all as glad to have Matthew home as I am. He still has his big white-sox chestnut horse. When I saw him coming up the road to pick me up, it still gave me heart palpitations just as it used to in the beginning of our courtship. If anything, he is more dear and handsome than ever and more dearly beloved.

Sitting on the buggy seat beside him also seemed like old times. He even drove a mile out of his way, out to the Millstream Orchards, where the lilac bushes are now blooming! This time he didn't pick armfuls to twine into the horse's bridle and harness. With his pocketknife, he clipped off just a small lovely bouquet to pin on my cape. It gave off such a sweet scent and made me feel special.

At the Bontragers' I was reminded anew of what a dear and precious family they are! The little boys have grown so. I can't imagine Benuel running to me and calling me Dolly now anymore. He'd rather hide behind his mother's skirts. David is no longer a baby either, and he hardly seemed to know me anymore.

Rosabeth and I had an old-time sisterly chat, just as I do with Sadie. I feel blessed indeed when I think of having her as a future sister-in-law.

We had a delicious supper. Everyone did their best to make me feel right at home, just like one of the family. They have a reason to rejoice, now that their prayers for Matthew's homecoming have been answered. I can tell that they are all (especially Daed Isaac and Mamm Rosemary) thankful from the depths of their hearts.

The ride home was also memorable, in the fragrantly scented evening air, with the birds still warbling good-night to each other. We have so much to talk about now and plans to make, but sometimes companionable silence is just as good or better than talking.

I'm holding Baby Alpheus as I write because he was quite fussy for awhile tonight. I offered to walk the floor with him in place of Betty, so she can get some rest. Now he has fallen asleep with his head on my shoulder, a precious little bundle indeed. I think I'll copy something out of *Gold Dust* yet before I take him back downstairs.

Golden Gem for Today
*On no account neglect the duty you owe
to friendship, relatives, and society.
But reserve some part of each day
only for yourself and God.*

May 29

I had a letter from Mrs. Worthington today. As soon as Matthew and I get back to Pennsylvania, she wants us to come and visit her. She hasn't met my sweetheart yet, and I know she will be duly impressed. I'm anxious to show him to her (smiles). She wrote that she already has a wedding gift picked out for us; it sure wonders me what it might be!

Her letter was friendly and newsy and gave me *Heemweh* (homesickness) for seeing her again. I will content myself with writing her a long letter tonight.

Through the open window comes the poignant chorus of the frogs down in the run. The dusky twilight is falling over the lovely countryside. Enos and the boys are still out in the field, planting the last of the field corn. Oh, I see them coming in now with the horses, so they must be finished.

The saying goes that when the leaves of the white oak trees are as big as squirrels' ears, it's time for farmers to plant the corn, but this spring the season is a bit late. Another saying claims that if the oak leaves are out before the ash, summer comes with a splash, with wet weather. We are having a cool wet May, and that's supposed to bring much fruit and hay, according to the old-timers.

The peonies are blooming alongside the purple iris beds, giving a touch of color to the landscape. Flowers are food for the soul, cheering us on our way, just as they encouraged the weary pioneers traveling to the West. The birds, too, are happily singing every day, brightening our hearts as well. These wonders of God's creation remind us to count our blessings.

June 15

Matthew's employers, the Kendletons, came from California and are in the area. They spent a day with the Bontragers, visiting Matthew. Then in the evening they drove over here to take Matthew and me out to eat in a restaurant. This is quite different from our usual custom of having a picnic out in the yard or meadow.

The Kendletons have capable help on their farm now — two brothers who once operated a farm themselves. They finally were able to go on "a much-needed vacation," as they expressed it. They presented us with wedding gifts in advance: a set of fine silverware for me to put into the chest Matthew made for me for Christmas, and a tool chest filled with a lot of useful tools for Matthew.

They took us to a fancy restaurant, with elegant tables, centerpieces, linen tablecloths, and shiny table settings. We each had a menu card and could order whatever we wished. We ordered steak, mashed potatoes, and vegetables, what we are used to eating at home. The steaks and mashed potatoes were delicious, but the vegetables weren't as good as our homegrown ones.

Choosing from the wide variety of fancy desserts was harder, for everything looked irresistible. The Kendletons insisted on paying for our meals. It must have cost them about as much as we spend for a week's worth of groceries. We didn't know we were supposed to leave a tip for the waitress until we were back home and

Enos told me. I hope the Kendletons handled that when they paid the bill. Without tips, waitresses are underpaid, Enos said.

On the way home, Mrs. Kendleton asked if we'd like to stop at a store and do some shopping. We decided that it would be a good time to pick out a clock at the jeweler's. We chose a wall clock with a swinging pendulum (Matthew's gift to me). He told me that we'll take it as a symbol of our engagement, just like a ring is to the *Englischer* (non-Amish person).

Then we went to the dry goods store and chose the fabric for my wedding dress. Now I'm excitedly waiting for a rainy or not-so-busy day, to give me time to sew it. I should have done it last winter when I was helping Mrs. Worthington, but at that time we didn't have our wedding date set yet.

I have the clock on the wall in my room here at Enos's place, awaiting the day when Matthew and I can have it in our own kitchen. It's five months away now — our wedding date. So it's high time for us to find a place to live. We wouldn't want to let it go until the last minute.

We're hoping that by spring a farm will come up for rent in this community. The Millstream Orchards Farm would be our first pick. But if it doesn't become available, another one would do just as well.

I think I'll take time to copy a bit out of *Gold Dust* yet, before I sink my weary bones into bed, aching because it's strawberry picking time.

Golden Gem for Today
*If we burden ourselves with countless prayers,
carelessly and mindlessly repeated
from impatience to finish them,
it interferes with our meditations.
Such praying wearies, torments, and dries
up the soul, hindering the work
of the Holy Spirit.*

June 21

I have a bouquet of red rambler roses on my bureau. Outside my window Mrs. Jenny Wren is trilling sweetly and continuously from the vines climbing the porch trellis. Wrens are one of my favorite songsters, and I'm so glad they chose this spot.

Best of all, I have chubby little Alpheus here in my arms. He was a bit fussy, and his mom needed a break. The girls were outside doing their chores and not available. He's smiling and cooing now, as I fuss over him, but I don't know how long it will last.

I see that in my last entry I forgot to explain why I'm still here at Enos Millers' home. That ten acres of produce made them busier than they had planned. Besides, they knew I would be glad for the chance to stay here in this community, now that Matthew's back. Yes, I am thankful, but I think I should keep my eyes open for something else to do for the rest of the summer. Soon there should be a lull in the work.

July 2

Today I finally found some time to cut and sew my wedding dress while Enos and most of the boys went to a horse sale, and Enos Jr. had to do some hoeing in the garden. Last week I told Betty that I'd like the chance to sew my wedding dress soon. I knew she would be careful to keep it a secret, but with the children, it might be another story. I don't know if they would be able to keep from telling others.

Besides, they'd be sure to tease me a lot (though not unkindly) the rest of the time I'm here. They suspect, though, that we're getting married this fall. If they'd have seen me sewing a dress in the summertime, when we are busy with gardens and canning, they'd surely have guessed what it was for.

Betty and the younger children went to the store this afternoon, so I was alone in the kitchen, happily and peacefully sewing away in midafternoon. Then the door opened and someone came into the enclosed porch. I jumped up, grabbed every piece and scrap of fabric, and ran into the *Sitzschtubb* (sitting room) with it, in the nick of time. Enos Jr. walked into the kitchen just as I disappeared through the other door.

Back in the kitchen, I tried to act nonchalant, and he suspected nothing. We had a nice chat before he had to go and hoe weeds in the cornfield again. He has a calf he's bottle feeding, and he knows where all the birds' nests are. Young Enos reminds me a lot of Owen's Milo (who is dating Matthew's sister Anna Ruth), even though Enos is younger and the two are not more closely related than second cousin.

This reminds me: at our wedding, Milo and Anna Ruth might get the job of being *Newesitzer* (groomsman and bridesmaid, witnesses). I'm sure they'll all enjoy traveling to Pennsylvania. Matthew says his parents and brothers and sisters are looking forward to the wedding and having a chance to visit friends and relatives back home.

Once again we've turned a calendar page, bringing the big day that much closer. Ya, well, the baby is getting fussy, and I think I'll take him outside for a little walk, maybe stopping at the barn to see the stock. There's a feeling of peace and contentment at this time of the day, when the lovely twilight is filtering down over the countryside and farm, and birds are twittering their good-night songs. May we remember to give thanks to the Creator.

July 11

I've landed myself a job, right here within a half mile of Enos Millers' place, on the Millstream Orchards Farm. When Matthew and I were exploring the place that Sunday evening, we had no idea that someone still did live there: Miss Sophie, a thin old lady ninety years old. She broke her hip and had surgery, then spent six weeks at an old people's home.

Her insurance only paid for six weeks there, and she didn't have the money to stay longer. So Jane, a friend of hers, came to her aid, helped her to find a "nurse" (me), and brought her home. She's a dear, tiny little old lady, with a lacy set of wrinkles, silvery white hair, and snapping black eyes.

Miss Sophie has a mind of her own, and it's still really good. She spends her days on the wheelchair and on her rocker. She told me she could have sold her farm, and would have had enough money to probably spend the rest of her life at the nursing home, but she preferred to come home. This is the only home she's ever known. I can't blame her for wanting to come back to familiar surroundings, even though they're old and worn.

Everything in this house seems incredibly old. The ancient linoleum is worn through, the woodwork looks like it hasn't been painted for fifty years, and the wallpaper is faded and hanging loose at a lot of places. There's an old two-toned Columbian cookstove in the kitchen that she still uses in the winter. The entire house smells musty, and the curtains and rugs are likely moth-eaten.

I explored the place, from the cellar to the old cupola on top, and realized that this house was at one time a grand place. It could be made beautiful again. Outside there are beds of poppies and daisies nearly overgrown with weeds, and a few scraggly shrubs here and there. I'm taking a keen interest in everything because of the possibility that the place might come up for rent next spring, and we might get first chance.

A farmer over the hill had been tilling the land for years, but rumors are out that he doesn't want it any longer. I haven't asked Miss Sophie about it, but soon I intend to do so. Meanwhile, I'll do all I can to make this place look better, whether or not we'll have a chance living here.

I'm in my bedroom now, the room adjoining Miss Sophie's room, so I'll be able to hear her call if she needs me during the night. My room was depressingly drab until I made curtains for the windows, put a pretty bedspread on the bed, and laid down a large throw rug to cover the unsightly linoleum. Before doing anything else, I thoroughly cleaned everything, of course.

The first few nights I was here, the squirrels' antics kept me awake as they scuffled around on the attic floor above me. By now, I'm getting used to it. I'll have to ask Enos how we can get rid of them. I miss the Millers and the lively children. But I believe if I keep myself busy, I'll be able to survive here for two months. September is the month I've planned to go back home so I can prepare for our wedding!

July 17

My days are falling into a pattern. In the morning I bathe and dress Miss Sophie, help her into her wheelchair, then cook our breakfast. She doesn't eat sugary cereal out of a box. No ma'am! She wants cooked oatmeal with wheat bran. She says she believes she has eaten oatmeal for breakfast every morning since she was a baby.

Then, after the kitchen is tidied, I roll her wheelchair outside on the porch, where she can watch me as I work. I scythed and stacked piles and piles of tall weeds in the garden; I hoed and pulled numerous smaller weeds. Next I cleaned the yard of twigs and branches and scythed it and mowed it. Then I cleaned the old neglected flower beds, arranged a border of rocks around each one, and mulched them. I even trimmed the overgrown lilac bushes way back.

Betty and the little girls walked over to visit us last night. She couldn't get done exclaiming about how much better the place already looks! Miss Sophie asked to hold Baby Alpheus. It was an exquisite experience for her.

She said she hadn't held a little baby for over forty years! I had been wondering whether Miss Sophie was a churchgoer when she was still able, but I didn't have the courage to ask her. So I was glad when Betty asked her if she is a Christian and was amused at her quick reply: "Oh, heavens, yes! And I have been for all of eighty-eight years!" She is such a chipper old soul, even though her outward body is fragile.

On Sunday Miss Sophie's friend Jane sat with her while I went to church. In the evening when Matthew came, there wasn't a nice-enough room to sit in. So after I put Sophie to bed, we spent much of the evening outdoors, roaming over the whole farm. We explored the orchards, the spruce stand, the ponds, and the fields.

Then we came back to the house so I could check on Miss Sophie. She was resting but not yet sleeping and said she was okay. So we sat on a fallen log by the pond, watching the moon and stars coming out. Just then, right before our eyes, in the deepening twilight, a doe and fawn walked around the pond. Every now and then, they paused to roll their bright and alert eyes this way and that, scanning the place for danger.

We could hear coyotes howling eerily from far off in the hills. I could almost imagine myself Idella McNeil, traveling west, sitting by a campfire near the covered wagons. I would be watching the moon rise and hearing the timber wolves howl.

Ya, well, Miss Sophie finally fell asleep now, after being restless for several hours. I'd better head for bed, too. I'll take the time to copy an inspirational verse yet.

Golden Gem for Today
Sometimes the world seems to turn against us.
People mistake our motives and words.
A dark look or cutting word
shows us the feelings of others,
who icily reject our friendly advances.
How hard it all seems,
especially when the cause is unknown!
Have courage and patience, dear one!
God is making a furrow in your heart,
where he will sow his grace.
Injustice or slights, patiently borne,
often leave the heart filled with marvelous
joy and peace
by the close of the day.
It is the seed God has sown,
springing up and bearing fruit.

Miss Sophie is such a dear, affectionate old soul. Matthew came over on Wednesday evening to ask her about renting the farm. When he shook hands with her, she held onto his hand for the longest time, utterly fascinated. One would almost have thought he was her boyfriend instead of mine!

When he asked her the question, she sat there, unblinking for a few minutes, still holding his hand. Then she said saucily, "No way will I rent my farm to you. Why, I wouldn't even think of doing so!" She let that sink in for awhile, then added, "I don't have close relatives still alive, so I'll will it to you two, that is, if you'll take care of me in my old age. Is that a deal?"

What a deal! When does she expect her old age to begin, after she becomes a centenarian? It shouldn't be so many years any more. But we would gladly care for her until she's 120, in exchange for the farm.

We accepted her offer and thanked her graciously, still not quite believing our blessing! There will be a lot of hard work ahead, but the place can eventually be made presentable, as we apply ourselves and elbow grease. I already have big ideas of what I want to do with the house to make things look better. Matthew and I stood at the gate, talking and planning with growing excitement, until the moon was high in the sky!

August 3

Cory's Paint and Wallpaper Store had a closeout sale last week. I badly wanted to go, so I called Miss Sophie's friend Jane to stay with her again. I made a trip to the city and came home with gallons and gallons of paint, and boxes and boxes of rolls of wallpaper in discontinued styles.

The wallpaper was at giveaway prices because it's not the washable, prepasted vinyl that everyone else wants these days, but the old-fashioned kind no longer made. But for me, that's easier to handle and put on the walls anyhow, though I don't like to do it by myself. Luckily none of it has to be matched; it's all in fine prints. It will serve its purpose to make this house look half decent until we can afford better.

Enos and Betty kindly sent the three oldest boys over to help. We donned old clothes and started to paint woodwork right away. Luckily, little scraping or sanding needed to be done because it

hadn't been painted for ages and was down to bare wood. A whisk with a wire brush was usually all it needed.

Matthew and Rosabeth are planning to come over whenever it suits them to help hang the wallpaper. We aim to give this old place a complete face-lift, as economically as possible, so it will be fit for us to move into next spring. We feel so blessed to have this opportunity — it's an answer to prayer.

The farm is big enough that Enos can still rent his ten acres for farming produce, so everyone should be happy. In September we plan to have a work bee to get the barn ready for cows. Everything is falling into place so nicely, or so it seems to us. Miss Sophie is delighted with all the activity and says she's glad her old home won't be going into strangers' hands.

She's getting sprier every day, with the therapy I'm giving her morning, noon, and night. The first week I was here, a visiting nurse came out and taught me how to do it. Then twice a day, we also have a practice session using her walker. That's going better than it did at first, too.

Miss Sophie sleeps a lot better, now that her hip is mending and doesn't pain her much anymore. With her spicy wit and charm, she's a delight to take care of. But it all makes me quite busy: by evening I'm bone weary, but with a satisfying tiredness of having accomplished a lot.

I'm sitting on the old porch steps now, looking down over the old orchards and tangled woodland. The misty twilight is fast falling over the peaceful countryside. Crickets are chirping cheerfully, and a sliver of a moon is rising over the treetops. Time to stop; it's getting too dark to see what I'm writing.

August 12

Nearly every day this week, Matthew and Rosabeth were here, helping to paper the rooms. I can hardly believe how much we got done and how much better it looks — so clean and fresh! Another week of work should wind it up. Then we just have to do something with the floors. Matthew tore out most of the worn and tattered linoleum. Now the floors are waiting for new coverings.

Miss Sophie's friend Jane told us that a friend of hers from the city owns a motel. He's taking out all the carpeting, still in good shape, and replacing it with new. There'll be a whole truckload of rolls of used rugs that someone could have for free. We thanked her for offering it, but told her we can't have wall-to-wall carpeting. It's against the *Ordnung* (church rules).

I suppose we'll have to buy linoleum, but we want to wait till the paperwork on the farm is done and the agreement signed. Miss Sophie's lawyer is on vacation. As soon as he gets back, we'll make an appointment.

I surely enjoyed this past week and look forward to the next. Having Matthew and Rosabeth here is lots of fun. It even makes the distasteful (to me) task of putting up wallpaper seem like fun.

I've heard that if a couple can hang wallpaper together, they will hang together. We passed this classic test of a marriage with flying colors — wallpaper colors, that is. There's no doubt that Matthew will be a jewel of a husband. I hope I can be worthy of him.

Time for an inspirational verse:

Golden Gem for Today
Nothing so elevates the soul as prayer.
God comes down to the soul and
raises it with him
to the regions of light and love.

Then, the prayer finished, the soul returns
to daily duties with a refreshed mind
and a steadier will.
The soul is filled with radiance divine
and sheds some of its abundance
upon neighbors.

August 18

Here in Miss Sophie's kitchen, the view from the window is out over the lilac bushes. I envision them next spring, covered with clouds of fragrant lavender blossoms. Matthew and I will be sitting at our cozy little table for two, with the sweet fragrance of the blossoms wafting in on the breeze through the open window.

I'll put some pretty shelf edging on the shelf on the west wall. There we'll put Clark's stagecoach and horses set, and above it on the wall, we'll put our new clock. We will be busy but very happy; happiness always surrounds us when each lives for the other and both live for God.

I build dream castles in the air until I'm brought back to earth to the mundane things that need to be done. Today I painted the old chipped and rusty enamel kitchen cabinets. The fresh coat of white paint made them look so much better, but

I dream of someday having splendid, L-shaped, Amish-made oak kitchen cabinets, with a gleaming Formica top.

Oh, well, we can't have everything right away. It's the love that counts in a home, not the furniture or the elegance of the house. If there would be no love, these things wouldn't make us a bit happier anyway.

I had a letter from sister Sadie today. Though she herself doesn't realize it, she's a paragon of unselfish love, always doing kind and helpful things for others. Her life is rich in love even though she doesn't have a beau. There are many kinds of love in this world. Her generous, unselfish, loving heart reaps love in return, and her life is blessed. I wish I could be more like her.

August 27

It's hard to believe that dear old Miss Sophie is really gone — gone from this life forever. She just simply "fell asleep" with a lingering smile on her face. What a blessed way to go. We all attended her funeral yesterday, and now I am back at Enos Millers' farmhouse.

In a few weeks, or as soon as a vanload goes that way, I'll be heading homeward.

I'll help with the late summer canning and harvesting and get ready for the wedding. I'm really looking forward to spending a few months with my parents yet, before I leave them for good.

Matthew was here, at Enos's place for supper last night, after the funeral. In the evening we went for a walk in the dusky twilight, both feeling sad and shaken, taking turns to try to cheer each other up. It wasn't just because of the departure of Miss Sophie. She had a lived a good long life and deserved her rest. But the fact weighed on us that nothing had been done about transferring the farm to us.

Her lawyer hadn't returned and nothing was signed. Ever since I first started working there, I'm sure Miss Sophie hadn't made a new will or changed an old one. That means the farm will probably be sold at a public sale, and we won't get a chance at it because our savings are still too meager. Uncle Sam will likely get her money since she has no living relatives or descendants.

I have to wonder, why, oh why, couldn't she have lived just a few weeks longer? Why did our dream have to dissolve into thin air? At the supper table last night, Enos reminded us that someday we may look back and thank God for his leading in this matter. God's timing is always perfect, and his ways are higher than ours. So we are trying to accept it as God's will, hoping and praying that something else will turn up for us.

August 31

Sunday evening we had our date here in Betty's parlor, but it was such a beautiful evening that we decided to go for a stroll. We hadn't really planned where to go and then found ourselves automatically turning in the lane at the Millstream Orchards place. Maybe it was to say good-bye to it forever. We talked about all the work we had done on the place, and what we had spent. Oh, well, someone will benefit from it, I suppose. At least we hadn't spent money on the linoleum yet.

It was an enchanting evening, too enchanting for us to dwell on our troubles. We tried not to think about how we would soon be hundreds of miles apart again when I go back home to Pennsylvania. A harvest moon rose over the treetops. Night birds murmured sleepily as a breeze stirred leaves on the roadside birch trees, setting them to whispering and sighing. We didn't talk much, for the handwork of the Lord was awesome, and sometimes silence is more meaningful than words.

We saw a rosy glow in the west. An evening star shone above the shadowy treetops on the mist-blue mountains. The chorus of crickets heralded the coming of autumn. But this is one time we won't bemoan summer slipping away, for we look forward to our special day.

We're trusting that, somewhere or other, an opportunity will open for us, if not at farming, then in some other occupation. Matthew will be watching the ads in the farm paper. Almost every year, at least a few farms come up for rent, so we're not worried yet.

It would be nice to live close to Mamm and Daed, too, back in my home community. I'm getting excited about going home to them, and to Sadie and the boys. It seems so long since I've seen them all. I'll cherish those few months of living with them before I leave permanently to bloom in a home of my own with Matthew.

I unearthed my *Prayer Book for Earnest Christians* from the bottom of my drawer. I think I'll read a few prayers in it before I go to bed. Maybe I'll even find one about marriage.

Wedding Season in Pennsylvania

September 9

This finds me back at home in my dear, familiar room, which feels so homey and comfortable. I'm sitting on my old perch on the chest by the window. From here, I can see Mamm and Daed relaxing in lawn chairs by the rock garden after a busy day. Sadie is still weeding flower beds, though it must surely be too dark for her to see right.

The boys aren't back yet from helping Rudy fill his silo. As soon as they're back, we plan to go for a boat ride. It seems like ages since we've last done that, and there are only a few more days left in this summer.

Oh, good! Here come Priscilla and

Henry to pay us a visit, just like old times, so I must scoot!

September 15

Only two more months until the big day! It's hard to believe, though, in the midst of this heat wave, rather unusual for this time of year. Heat lightning is flickering tonight in the northwest sky, and the night insects are calling in the thickening twilight. According to the calendar, autumn is here, but it surely doesn't feel like it yet.

We haven't had much rain yet this month. The silo filling was early, for the cornstalks were dry and ready to be harvested. We're finished, and I suppose the sound of our *englisch* (non-Amish) neighbors' harvesters will soon be silent, too, and all the silos and trenches will be filled for another year.

We finally had a chance to have our boat ride on Saturday evening, with our whole family together, maybe for the last time. It was so enjoyable, floating peacefully on the water, with a silvery moon rising up over Grandpa Dave's barn. A caressing breeze was frolicking and dancing among the leaves, which are growing old and worn. They'll soon be changing color, to golds and reds and browns, and then gently floating down on the breeze, onto the water.

We reminisced about old times and old memories. I wondered how I would ever be able to leave them all, never to come back again as a belonging member of the household.

I think I'll copy a prayer out of my prayer book yet tonight, to remind me of spiritual blessings.

O holy triune God in heaven, rich in love!
We pray from our whole heart,
first and foremost.
Build us up and plant us
according to your holy will.
Convert us and draw us graciously to you.
Help us to obey you gladly and willingly,
to serve you and follow you in the ways
of your commandments.

October 4

Today was another busy one. Sometimes I wonder if we'll ever get ready. In one more month, Matthew will be coming! That will give him time to help us prepare for the wedding and to line up a carpenter job here for the winter. Even if an opportunity to rent a farm would come up, we wouldn't move on it until spring.

Matthew will board with Rudy's family until the wedding. Then on weekends after marriage, we'll do our *hochzichlich* (postwedding) visiting with the relatives. Even though our upcoming marriage hasn't been published yet at church, everyone that we consider "family" knows about it, such as Priscilla and Henry, Grandpa Daves, and Barbianne and Rudy.

My dear family has pitched in to help and can be counted on to assist some more, whenever the need arises. Mamm and Sadie are real troopers. Daed and the boys do all they can, too. I think we'll get ready.

October 21
___

There's a pleasant stir of excitement around the place that deepens as the big day gets closer. We were glad for all the Indian summer weather in which to do all the necessary painting and repapering. I don't think I'll ever again want to hang another piece of wallpaper or dip a brush into paint. Phooey! I'm tired of it, after doing so much of it at Miss Sophie's house. It's just not the same without Matthew to work with!

Tonight I'm wondering if I'm really ready for that all-important big step, out of young maidenhood and into another walk of life, to be a wife to Matthew. The closer it gets, the more qualms I seem to be having. Maybe if Matthew were here, it would be different. But as of now, he's still hundreds of miles away.

At other times, my inner butterflies are gone, and I am ready and willing to leave Father and Mother, ready to go to the ends of the earth with Matthew, if necessary. I look forward to having a home of our own and doing my own housekeeping. I'm not the least bit worried that Matthew won't be kind and considerate. I'm sure we'll be forgiving of each other's faults.

Golden Gem for Today
Two hearts separated by distance
can pray at the same hour
with the same words.
This soothing prayer each day reunites
those two sad hearts torn
by the agony of parting.
In God's presence, they are strengthened
by the same Holy Spirit and recover courage
to tread the road to heaven,
together in heart though apart in body.

Matthew is here! Mere words won't do much to express my feelings, so I won't even try. I hope I've written my last letter to him and that we'll never be parted by miles again. In just a few days, we'll be published, and the whole church will know of our plans.

A few flakes of snow are falling tonight, making it seem like November and winter. I'm glad our Indian summer weather is over. Somehow it just didn't seem like wedding season yet.

Now it does! The housecleaning upstairs is finished, but the whole first floor must be done yet. We have to bake and frost twenty cakes, make crocks and crocks of pudding, and fry, sugar, or fill hundreds of doughnuts. But I'm not really worried, for we'll have lots of help.

If it weren't for Sadie, though, maybe I would be anxious. She shoulders the work around here, while I find myself scatter-brained and subject to fits of daydreaming. Sadie gave me a beautifully patterned, finely stitched plain top quilt for a wedding gift. That fills my hope chest to the brim, along with Mamm's rugs and the quilts I made while at Mrs. Worthington's.

My new furniture is all ordered from an Amish craftsman and should be finished by spring. It's hard to plan, not knowing yet to where we'll move, but we're trusting that something will turn up.

A week ago we sent a wedding invitation to Mrs. Worthington and Clark. Today we received a reply: she and Clark are planning to come! I hope they'll enjoy their day and won't think us crude. One thing is sure, it will be quite different from a Quaker wedding.

November 6

Matthew spent the evening here last night. After the others had gone to bed, we sat and talked longer than we'd been intending to, until the fire burned low on the grate. We don't know yet where our home of dreams will be, but we can still talk about it and the lofty ideals we have for it.

I found a sweet poem that I'll copy here. I've seen it in a different version, but I like this one best:

My Kingdom

I'm queen of a beautiful kingdom;
God gave it to me for my own.

167

My castle is a rambling old farmhouse,
With a low rocking chair for my throne.
My subjects are dear little children
Who willingly come at my call.
The king is the husband and father,
Who furnishes bread for us all.

I gladly will mend little stockings,
Or hear a short prayer at my knee.
I marvel that God in his wisdom
Presented this kingdom to me.

I often feel weak and unworthy
To guide little footsteps that roam,
To keep them all safe and contented
In our beautiful kingdom of Home. (anon.)

I hope and pray that God will give me such a beautiful kingdom someday, a home filled with childish voices, echoing with laughter, singing, and love. A home with sweet, innocent babies to love and care for; lovable little tykes for me to rock, comfort, and kiss their hurts away. A home where I kneel with the children at bedtime, hear their lisping prayers, and tuck them into their beds.

I hope for a home where babies with little unsteady feet toddle after us as we go about our work, their little arms lifted up to us to be held and hugged. A home filled with the music and childish laughter and prattle of loving adorable children, more cherished than any earthly possession.

The Bible says, "Lo, children are an heritage of the Lord; . . . happy is the man who has his quiver full of them." That's my secret dream, that Matthew and I will have our heritage of children.

November 10

Matthew's parents and all of his brothers and sisters have arrived. They're doing some visiting in this community, both before and after the wedding. Milo and Anna Ruth will be *Newesitzer* (groomsman and bridesmaid), seated on Matthew's side, and Peter and Sadie will be *Newesitzer* on my side.

We also sent an invitation to Owen and Lizzie Hershberger, and to Enos and Betty Miller. But they all ruefully declined because of the miles between us and the difficulty of leaving their families for so long.

Matthew's dad brought us the news that Miss Sophie's farm has been sold to an outsider. I privately shed a few tears about it, for the hopes and dreams we'd built up for that place. We were imagining how we'd love it when the lilacs were blooming and the fragrant rambler roses were ablaze on the trellises. The rambling old wall would be covered with the sweetness of honeysuckle in blossom.

Oh, well, I don't doubt but that something else will turn up. There will be other flowers and birds, ponds and orchards, millstreams and spruce groves. We'll be together, no matter where. I suppose at first we won't mind so much where we live or how simple our home and furnishings. We'll live on the love that will sweeten our surroundings, be it in a castle or in a hovel.

November 14, Tuesday

Our household is all in a hurry-flurry, filled with wedding preparations. Matthew and the boys spent the day raking leaves from under all our trees around here. Some cousins are fetching the bench and supply wagons, for seating at our wedding on Thursday.

Tomorrow a bunch of neighbors will be here, butchering turkeys, baking, cooking, cleaning, and running errands. Others are making urgent trips to the store for supplies. I ironed my wedding dress and new *Kapp* (covering), pressed Matthew's new suit, polished our new shoes, and tried to calm the inner butterflies plaguing me.

Tonight I had an unexpected but pleasant surprise. A delivery truck drove in, and a man came to the door with a big bouquet of fragrant pink roses, sent by Mrs. Worthington. They make the whole kitchen look lovely and lend a lingering sweetness. Just for a few minutes, I caught myself wishing they'd be lavender lilacs. Roses are just as nice, likely imported, and quite expensive.

November 15, Wednesday

While Sadie and I were cubing bread for the filling, we had a good chat — something that will likely be more rare in the future. She is genuinely happy for us and assured me that Matthew will make a wonderful husband and that I will be the perfect wife for him. Trust Sadie to give a sincere compliment; no empty flattery for her!

Mamm Miriam also seems to be happy that her previously wayward and sometimes troublesome daughter has chosen a path that she approves of. She is sure that I will be in good hands.

Tonight Matthew and I took a tour of the house, to make sure everything is ready and nothing amiss or forgotten. With all the help we had, nothing should've been left undone! The rooms were spotless. Early tomorrow morning, the men will move much of the downstairs furniture out to a shed. They'll take out a movable partition around the first-floor master bedroom, and place the benches for the expected guests. The turkeys are ready to be roasted by the cooks, and the potatoes are all peeled.

Next we went down into the cellar to see if everything was okay there. The celery was cleaned and ready. Mamm had taken special care of it this fall, so it would be nicely bleached and crisp for this special occasion. The lavishly iced cakes made a pretty picture alongside the delicious-looking filled donuts. There were big crocks of butterscotch and vanilla pudding and fruit salad.

We saw rows of homemade bread ready to slice. The macaroni salad was in crocks in the basement refrigerator. Jars of green seven-day sweet pickles and colorful chow chow were on the shelf. The cheese was cubed and in big containers beside the pretzels and homemade noodles. There were jars of strawberry jelly and pounds of homemade butter.

Everything seemed to be ready and nothing forgotten. If only everything will go well for us now! The weather was cloudy, damp, and cold today. What will it be like tomorrow? Matthew was teasing me: "It looks like it could be a day of freezing rain and sleet, with treacherous roads."

Oh, dear, I hope not. What if no one would show up? Matthew reassured me, however: "As long as the bishop can come and we can get married, I won't be disappointed."

Dear Diary, don't expect me to write something in you tomorrow. I'll be too busy with our wedding and the celebrations!

It's time to get to bed and try to sleep. But first I want to read and meditate on a few prayers in my *Prayer Book for Earnest Christians*. I've been having some serious and reverent thoughts all day, about marriage and our new walk in life, the seriousness of this step, and the necessity of much prayer. I'm sure Matthew has been doing the same. I can find only one wedding prayer in it so I'll study that yet, and make it my own.

Our long-prepared-for big day has come and gone, but our journey on the pathway of matrimony has just begun. Today was a busy day, working to get everything back into its proper place. We packed and returned all the borrowed dishes. Matthew and the boys loaded the benches back into the bench wagon. Since our district has no church this coming Sunday, the benches were available for the next local bridegroom to come and haul them to his intended bride's home.

I must say that everything went well enough, thanks to the cooks, table waiters, hostlers (caring for the visitors' horses), ushers, dishwashers, and so on. We had over two hundred guests. Nobody went home hungry, or if they did, it was their own fault. The whole family pitched in to help today. Already the wedding gifts have all been packed and put into storage until spring.

The ministers' instructions to us upstairs in the counsel room and the wedding sermon itself — both were very meaningful to Matthew and me. This afternoon (with Matthew's help) I wrote down all I could remember of it in our "Wedding Mem-

There remain then faith, hope, love, these three; but the greatest of these is Love

1 Corinthians 13:13

ories" book. The encouragement and advice about having a Christian home and living in harmony made a deep impression on us. The ministers portrayed marriage at its best, in all its solemnity, holiness, and beauty.

I'm sure our voices trembled when we said our "Ya" in answer to the bishop's questions, but no one seemed to mind. I was thankful that it's not part of our custom to exchange rings or to kiss in front of all the guests.

The rest of the day was fun and easy. For the meal, Matthew and I were sitting at the *Eck* (corner) table, which was adorned with a beautiful cake and other fineries. In the afternoon, we and the guests were singing and visiting together.

For the less formal supper, each *Bu* (young man) chose a girl to sit with. Later in the evening, the *rumschpringers* (youths at least sixteen years of age and running around together) had their party games out in the barn.

Thus our big day passed by, a joyful event for which we had planned and worked so long. I'm thankful the weather cooperated as well as it did, though it wasn't all that nice. There was snow, not the kind where big, beautiful fluffy snowflakes come floating down, but the kind that is driven by the wind, with tiny hard little flakes coming from dreary skies. There wasn't much accumulation, though, so there was no danger of anyone getting stuck in a drift or stranded.

Mamm had been a little worried about heating this big, drafty farmhouse both upstairs and downstairs. A howling northwest wind would try to enter every time the doors opened. But with the wind from the east, there was no problem, and the house was cozily warm.

Daed said that when his uncle Peter got married, it snowed a lot the night before. On his way to the wedding, the drifts were so deep that his buggy overturned and he lost his hat in a drift. After searching for it, he had to go on without it.

I've heard of weddings that had to be postponed because of blizzards. So we still had a lot to be thankful for. An old saying claims that if it snows on your wedding day, you will get rich. I hope that means rich in love, for I wouldn't be satisfied merely to be rich in this world's goods.

I know there's nothing to that saying. Anyhow, I'd rather claim the traditional English rhyme:

If you wed in bleak November,
Only joys will come, remember.

Oh, oh, I hear a childish little voice from the hallway, calling Dolly, Dolly, so I must go. Little Benuel stayed with us today while his parents went visiting, and he quickly got over his shyness. I had almost forgotten that he used to call me that.

Matthew's out helping with the chores, and I suppose he will soon be in, so I'll have to hide my diary somewhere in a drawer. I suppose it's good that it's nearly filled. Then I'll pack it away in a trunk to reread years from now.

November 23, Thanksgiving Day

Our whole extended family was invited to Rudy and Barbianne's today for dinner. She served roasted turkey with all the trimmings, and a full course meal besides. It was a day of visiting and fellowship, a relaxing day after our stressful weeks of preparing for the wedding.

Matthew and I crossed the field to their place, walking through lazily falling snow. We haven't had much time alone yet. We talked of how nice it would be to move to our own home right away, instead of waiting until spring.

About the wedding and our guests — I have not yet written all that I want to put in my diary. Mrs. Worthington and Clark were there and seemed to have genuinely enjoyed the day. They thanked us profusely for inviting them. Both of them admired the meal so, and all the wedding gifts, and marveled at the number of guests.

Mrs. Worthington asked if she could take pictures, but we politely declined. It would've been hard for them to do so without catching people in the photos. That certainly would've displeased many of our people since one of our church rules is against it.

She said she had a wedding gift for us, but that we must come to her home to find out what it is. Mrs. Worthington will send us an invitation as soon as their new mansion is finished, which Grant insisted on rebuilding. She wants us to stay for several days.

Pamela Styer was invited, too, and she also enjoyed the wedding. She came over to help clean up the next day. While she was working with us, she apologized for something she'd said to Matthew and me when she greeted us in the line of well-wishers after the ceremony. After hearing the many wishes of *gute Glick* (good luck/ success) and blessings, it seemed strange (and we were surprised) to hear her saying, "May all of your troubles be little ones." Ya, well, I hope so, too. She means well.

Time to quit writing. Matthew will soon be done helping Peter feed the steers, and I want to get my diary out of sight before he comes in. Someday I'll show it to him, but not yet. In his wedding sermon, the bishop told us that we ought not to keep anything from each other. That sounds like good advice. I think I'll copy something out of *Gold Dust* yet.

Golden Gem for Today
Blessed is the united prayer of two friends,
bound together in holy friendship.
With desires and thoughts as one,
they present themselves before God.

December 4

I spent the day at Priscilla and Henry's house while Matthew was at his carpenter job. In the Old Testament times, when a man got married, he was to take a year off from distant traveling and stay at home to make his wife happy. Wouldn't that be nice for today's times, too!

I enjoyed my day helping Priscilla care for yet another family of little tykes that Children's Services has placed with them while their mother is in prison. The baby is only three months old but already has a whole head full of dark hair, plenty enough to make bobbies (plaited hair).

Her older sister is still a baby herself at fourteen months old; she has the biggest, darkest eyes I've ever seen. Their brother is two, and a regular *Nixnutz* (mischievous child), getting into everything. They're so cute and lovable, so dear and defenseless, and I have to wonder what crime their mother committed that she landed in prison.

I had my fill of rocking and cuddling babies today, singing lullabies, and crooning sweet tunes, all to my heart's content. Priscilla feels quite tied down, even with Miriam Joy's help. While I was there, she was glad to catch up on odd jobs that had been pushed aside. The baby keeps her up a lot at night, too. Yes, I know that being a mother isn't all coos, smiles, and patty-cakes, but still, I think it would be wonderful.

I'll copy part of the love chapter yet, before Matthew comes in from the shop where he and Crist are helping Peter on a woodworking project.

Love is very patient and kind,
never jealous or envious,
never boastful or proud,
never haughty or selfish or rude.
Love does not demand its own way.
It is not irritable or touchy.
It does not hold grudges
and will hardly even notice
when others do it wrong.
It is never glad about injustice,
but rejoices whenever truth wins out.
If you love someone you will be loyal to him
no matter what the cost.
You will always believe in him,
always expect the best of him,
and always stand your ground
in defending him.
(Paul, in 1 Corinthians 13:4-7, TLB)

This sounds like good advice for a marriage.

December 7

During the night a howling wind brought a heavy snowstorm down from wintry skies and covered our farm with beautiful, icy swirling drifts. This afternoon the sun came out brightly, though, and now a row of glittering, crystal-clear icicles hang from the porch roof.

The neighborhood children were sledding on Grandpa Dave's hill. They tramped down the snow to make a slide and poured water over it, to freeze into a smooth, slick run. Tonight Matthew and I took our toboggan and went for a spin, and it was great fun! The moon was rising in the east, and the cold air was clear and frosty. Millions of stars twinkled down at us.

It was a fast, thrilling ride down, but a slow walk back up. When we were tired, we trudged up to Grandpa Dave's house. As usual, Grandma Annie welcomed us cheerily at the door, and Dave called out that we were to bring our boots along in, so they'd be warm for the homeward trek. Annie bustled around, making hot chocolate and bringing a plate of cookies from the pantry.

Sitting in their dear, homey, old-fashioned kitchen started up my longing for a home of our own. I could see how contented and peaceful they are in their love-filled home, and I wished that spring would be closer. We still have no prospects of renting a farm. We believe something will turn up, but it's hard to be patient.

Annie and Dave never had any children of their own. That must've been hard for them to accept. Yet they still are having a happy, blessed life together, as far as I can tell.

Dave was in one of his storytelling moods tonight, and we certainly enjoyed being a captive audience. When we came home, Peter asked Matthew to help him figure out a difficult measurement in his woodworking shop. Meanwhile I came up to our room to write some more in my diary.

I found a little poem that someone had sent in to *Die Botschaft* (newspaper) that I want to copy. It made me eager to start building.

Women Build Homes

A house is built of bricks and stones,
of pillars, posts, and piers,
But a home is built of loving deeds
That stand a thousand years.

Men of the world build houses,
Halls and chambers, roofs and domes;
But the women of the world, God knows
That women build the homes. (anon.)

December 19

After all our cooking and baking, getting ready for the wedding and using up the leftovers, I thought we'd skip the usual pre-Christmas cookie baking and candy making. But not so Sadie. She's already made at least a dozen kinds of cookies and several kinds of dipped chocolate candy. Sadie gives all the neighbors plates full of goodies wrapped in Saran Wrap and decorated with colorful bows.

She and her friends get together to make oodles of fruit baskets, and take them to nursing homes and to the sick or bereaved or elderly in our community. Sadie also sends a lot of cards, and not just at Christmas time, to anyone she can think of who needs cheering up or encouragement. No wonder everyone likes her!

There's good skating this year on the creek, so Peter and Crist planned a skating party for the *Yunge* (youths) old enough for *rumschpringing* (running around with the young people). Matthew and I weren't invited. But they had a big bonfire going down by the creek, and we couldn't stay away. So we sneaked down and sat on a log in the shadows, watching them play crack the whip and tag. It looked like fun, and I asked Matthew if he wished he could join them. He replied, "Not at all."

Soon we came up to the warm kitchen. Our weekends are taken up with our *hochzichlich* (postwedding) visiting of relatives and friends, and soon already our first month of marriage will be over. We've planned not to buy gifts for each other this Christmas. They would just have to be put into storage anyway until we have a home of our own.

December 21

A happy bunch of carolers, the *Yunge* (youths), were out last night, traveling on straw-filled, horse-drawn wagons. They were going from place to place to bring cheer and good wishes.

Matthew and I were out tobogganing again when the *Yunge* came by. The sweet, age-old melodies drifted up the hill when they sang for Grandpa Daves. The frosty air radiated with gladness and the joy of God's unspeakable gift to the world as they sang,

> *Joy to the world, the Lord is come!*
> *Let earth receive her King;*
> *Let every heart prepare him room,*
> *And heav'n and nature sing.*
> (*Isaac Watts*)

The sweet strains of "Silent Night, Holy

Night" echoed back on the wind as they happily drove out the lane, their sleigh bells ringing.

December 28

These past few weeks, Mamm and I have been quilting for a lady in town who has a quilt shop. She has some people appliquéing for her, some piecing, some quilting, and others binding. In the summertime, tourists buy the quilts, and she also sends out orders by UPS.

A few weeks after New Year's Day, we plan to head out to Minnesota again, to Matthew's parents. We'll stay with them for several weeks while Matthew helps to do carpenter work in the barn, building more horse stalls, and so on. It's something they can do while the snow flies outside.

I'm looking forward to our stay at their home. It will almost seem like old times, only better, for these are happier days, and the bittersweet long-distance courtship all but forgotten.

December 29

Today we received a letter from Mrs. Worthington. She wants Matthew and me to visit her and stay for a few days in the new Winslow Manor! Grant has had it rebuilt (or replaced) and intends to take himself a wife in June! He has built a wing or suite of rooms for his mother. But the way it sounds, the place is so spacious that they won't even be close to each other.

Mrs. Worthington wants Clark to drive over for us the day after New Year's Day, and we can stay as long as we want! We're supposed to call her to say whether or not it suits us. We'd like to go, but I hope we won't feel too out of place to enjoy our visit. Perhaps we could even call it a honeymoon trip.

Now What?

January 1

The brand new year has begun, first calendar year of our married life. I suppose the dawning of a new year is a good time to take stock of our lives, searching our hearts for hidden sins and repenting of the same. We need to forget the mistakes and failures of the past that we're sorry for and strive to overcome, to become more Christlike, and to grow in grace.

It was really cold this morning (minus 10 degrees Fahrenheit), but without much snow on the ground. We had a New Year's dinner for all the clan. I cherished it as a day of precious memories. Soon we'll be hundreds of miles away from them all again. It's hard telling when we'll be back — maybe never to live here, just to visit.

Matthew is sitting here at the kitchen table with me, looking at the farm paper, with a bowl of hot buttered popcorn and a basket of juicy red apples in front of us. Peter and Crist are warming their feet on the open door of the bake oven, and munching on apples and popcorn, too. They just came back from skating, saying it's almost too cold and windy to be fun.

Yes, Matthew knows all about my diary now and is highly amused about it. Last night when we were getting ready for bed, our room was so icy cold that I asked him to get another comforter out of the chest. I forgot that I'd hidden my diary under that very comforter several days ago.

"What's this?" he asked, holding up my diary and beginning to page through it. I made a dive for it, but he held it up out of my reach. When he saw what it was, he began to read snatches of it aloud, just to tease me. Finally I gave it up and crawled under the covers in embarrassment.

Then he relented and apologized. When he humbly asked for permission to read it, I knew it would never do to say no. He was so interested in reading it, with many a chuckle, that he nearly froze himself, and then he finished the rest this morning.

Ya, well, I hope he never finds my *old* diary, the one where I'd written a lot of things about Gideon, and such foolishness. Matthew doesn't mind my lengthy ramblings and even said that it will be interesting for us to reread when we're old. I want to copy something out of *Gold Dust* yet, and then it's bedtime.

Golden Gem for Today
You who no longer have a mother to love you,
and yet crave for love,
God will be as a mother.

You who have no brother to help you,
and have so much need of support,
God will be your brother.

You who have no friends to comfort you,
and stand so much in need of consolation,
God will be your friend.

January 4

Here we are in the spacious, elegant new Winslow Manor. I have to wonder what Idella McNeil would say if she could see it now, with all the inventions that came since her day: electricity, telephones, dishwashers, clothes washers and dryers, and other push-button gadgets to do the work.

Mrs. Worthington is a gracious hostess, and the food she serves is exotic and gourmet. She had Clark take us out to eat twice, and she went along, too. Then she took us on a tour of several museums and art exhibits, and on a shopping spree.

We spent our mornings in Clark's work-shop. Matthew really enjoyed that part, working with wood and hearing about the old Underground Railroad station. In the evening we took the opportunity to be alone on long walks around the winding drives near Winslow Manor, while Mrs. Worthington watched her television. It's grand around here, but I'm glad we're going home tomorrow. We have no real work to do here. Who would want to sit around and have Sunday all the time?

It's nice, though, to have a room that's cozy warm, with an adjoining bathroom. For sleeping, we have the biggest bed I ever saw, surely what they call a king size. Everything in this house is soft, easy, warm, and plush. This feature is rather nice for a change, but we're both glad to be getting back to the simple, common life.

Clark will be taking us home in his Cadillac. I expect that our old farmhouse and windmill and barn will be a dear and welcome sight. Just as I thought, Mrs. Worthington thinks the world and everything of Matthew. She said the wedding gift she plans to give is as much for him as for me. Just before we left, she said what it is: an all-expenses-paid trip to the Bahamas for a week! All we have to do is say when.

We didn't want to hurt her feelings and told her we'll think it over, but we already know we won't accept it! It just does not fit our way of living.

January 19

Dear Diary, guess what I was doing today! Teaching school in my old Birch Hollow School! So I guess I'm the Birch Hollow schoolmarm again, at least for a week. We arrived here at Matthew's parents' place on Friday. On Saturday morning word came to us that Becky Yoder has a bad case of tonsillitis and needs a substitute for about a week.

It seemed just like old times! The children's cheery "Good morning!" gave me a good feeling, just like it always used to do. Their bright and eager faces gave my heart a pang of *Heemweh* (homesickness) for my old schoolmarm days. They sang with such gusto that the little schoolhouse fairly rang with music. Then they recited their lessons with a will.

I can see that Becky has them well in line; the school isn't lacking in order and discipline. I bustled around, feeling schoolteacherish again, responding to raised hands, checking papers, and giving assignments. Little first-grader Freddie fell and skinned his knee and came in crying. By the time I was finished doctoring it up with a bandage and tape, he was smiling through his tears.

Mary Anne and Linda, Matthew's sisters, walked with me both to and from school. They chattered all the way, while I gazed in awe at the beauty of the snow-covered fields all around us. The splendid pine trees were laden with snow, their branches drooping nearly to the ground. This morning the air was so frosty cold that it made our cheeks quite rosy, but by tonight it had mellowed. I look forward to our daily walks together. I know I'll like being Birch Hollow schoolmarm for a week if all goes as well as it did today.

Matthew and I, with his parents, had a discussion tonight on what we should do if no farm becomes available by spring. The closer it gets, the harder it is not to worry. What options do we have?

His mother said we could always rent a small place, and Matthew could work as a day laborer. Yet jobs out here aren't as easy to find as they are back home, and this is where we had chosen to live. So we'll keep on praying and having faith, and accept whatever happens as God's will.

January 21

Matthew and I were invited to Owen Hershbergers' for supper. Matthew picked me up at the schoolhouse where I'd spent an hour correcting workbooks. He was driving in a one-horse sleigh! The roads were slick and icy this morning, so he took the scholars and me to school on that sleigh. Most of the school dads brought their children on sleighs, too.

Since Minnesota has so much snow, we adapt to it. It would never do to postpone school for a day just for a little snow and ice. It would have to be made up in the spring, when farmers are busy getting their fields ready for planting.

It seemed like old times, seeing Matthew's chestnut white sox come trotting up the road. I thought back to the times we picked lilac blossoms for decorating the horse's bridle and a choice sprig for my cape front. It brought back happy memories. I wonder where we'll be when the lilacs are blooming this May.

Supper was ready when we arrived at Owen's place. The whole family was already gathered in the kitchen. Daadi Milo had pushed Mammi Mattie, in her wheelchair, from their *Daadihaus* end of the farmhouse. I couldn't believe how much Baby Mary had grown! It hurt me that she didn't know me anymore and clung to her mother and sisters when I came near.

We had apple pie for dessert. Owen Jr. asked me if I remember the time we had rhubarb pie that should've been cut with an axe. The big table was so long that I don't think his dad, at the other end of the table, heard. I got him back by reminding him of the time we traded work for the day, and how it wasn't what he thought it would be after all.

The whole experience brought back a lot of memories: the scare we had from Baby Mary eating mice poison, little Lizzie catching her arm in the washing machine wringer, Daadi Milo drilling a hole in his toenail, the horses running off with a load of broccoli, Daadi dumping Mammi out of her wheelchair, and Lizzie being missing till we found her underneath a driving horse, but unharmed.

It seems there's never a dull moment in such a big family. I hope someday Matthew and I have just as many children. Daadi Milo and Daed Owen are both born talkers and storytellers, so we were royally entertained. Mamm Lizzie had prepared a scrumptious meal. We did justice to it because we were extra hungry after driving through the cold and snow. I copied a few of her recipes for my recipe box. The time slipped away and suddenly it was time for us to head for home.

It was a delightful evening. The sleigh ride home was exhilarating, with the frosty wind biting our noses. But we were snuggled together warm and cozy under the furry robes. The stars twinkling in the clear sky overhead seemed so close that we felt like we could almost reach up and get one. It was an awesome feeling, and God seemed very close.

I have my *Gold Dust* handy, so I'll copy a bit yet while I wait for Matthew to come in.

Golden Gem for Today
Simple piety, full of faith,
is like some good angel
overshadowing us with snowy wings,
showing us God everywhere,
in all, and with all.

January 23

Matthew's parents received an exciting letter yesterday from an uncle and aunt, Cephas and Barbara Bontrager, who live in a small settlement of our people in Belize (in Central America), earlier called British Honduras. They have no children of their own and have been running a small orphanage there. Now they've written a letter

saying that their helpers (a husband and wife team) wish to return to the United States sometime this year. So they're looking for others to take their place.

Cephas and Barbara are reaching old age and can't operate the orphanage by themselves anymore. They're looking for an adventurous couple who would be willing to come down for a year or so. Even just a half year would be better than nothing.

Matthew and I are immensely interested. Last night we sat and talked about it for a long time after the rest of the family had gone to bed. In the wee hours of the morning, we finally banked the fire and went to bed, to "sleep on it."

This morning the prospect seemed even more enticing than it did last night. I post-haste sent off a letter to Mamm and Daed, asking for advice and their blessings on the venture, if possible. Matthew's parents seem to feel it would be a good experience for us, a rewarding work to be in, caring for orphaned children. They say that Barbara and Cephas are a sincere and dedicated couple, and they would be a good influence on us.

I could hardly wait to finish my last day of being Birch Hollow schoolmarm so I could hurry home and discuss it some more with Matthew. We're both very excited about it. We both love children and think it would be a noble work.

February 3

It's all settled now. We've made the decision. Today we sent off that all-important volunteering letter to Uncle Cephas and Aunt Barbara!

It seems to us like God's leading, an answer to our prayer for guidance. My parents gave us their full blessing by mail. Now we're eagerly awaiting Barbara and Cephas's reply.

Something tells me that we're going. I just know they'll write and urge us to come.

It makes me a little sad to put all our lovely new furniture and wedding gifts into storage until we get back. Oh, well, the happiness of having a home of our own someday will be all the sweeter if it is deferred for awhile.

I have a feeling that we will be embarking on the greatest adventure of our lives and the most life-altering one. Last night I dreamed we were in Lancaster again and had brought back to Minnesota a sweet little baby girl! The dream did not tell me if she was our birth child or adopted. Either way, we loved her.

Since Mrs. Worthington insists on giving us an expensive wedding gift, we've decided to ask her to pay our ship fare to Belize instead of fare to the Bahamas, as earlier proposed. Then it would be a useful gift rather than one squandered in luxury and pleasure.

February 4

Just a few unfilled pages left in my diary. Mamm has sent me another one to fill, but I don't know if being a substitute mother for a bunch of orphaned children will allow any time for such writing. I'll probably be much too busy rocking babies!

Matthew and I went for another sleigh ride tonight, over to Enos and Betty Miller's for supper. We purposely went a bit early, so it wouldn't be dark yet, and took the long way around, past the Millstream Orchards Farm. We drove in and looked around a bit, feeling somewhat sad that our plans there had never come to fulfillment. The gnarled and twiggy old apple trees were loaded with ice and snow, and the pine branches drooped with the weight of their burdens.

A bright red cardinal flitted from branch to branch, adding a spot of color to the snowy scene. In front of the house, lilac bushes bravely stood sentinel, as if awaiting the warmth and awakening of life-giving spring weather. Against a background of swirled snow, the old stone mill made a scenic picture. The rambling stone honeysuckle wall was covered with mounds of snow all along its length.

We nodded a silent farewell, then sped away, and in a few minutes were turning in at the Miller lane. The warmth of Betty's big cheery kitchen certainly felt welcoming after our cold ride. She served a delicious supper, along with a jolly evening of reminiscing. What would life be without dear, kind friends?

The sleigh ride home in the frigid air topped off an enjoyable evening. We were feeling snug, covered up to the eyes with buggy robes, while watching a spectacular display of northern lights in the star-studded wintry sky. We watched in awesome wonder something of God's power displayed throughout the universe. The view put a song in our souls and our minds: "How Great Thou Art!"

"Man proposes, but God disposes." All our plans and anticipations for going south to Belize this spring are suddenly come to naught. A letter from Aunt Barbara and Uncle Cephas in yesterday's mail told us that our letter to them accepting the job had been delayed in the mail. So they supposed we weren't interested after all. In the meantime, another couple had taken the position for two years.

Aunt Barbara wrote that she has us down for after that, though, if we are still willing then. Well, we'll have to see what two years from now will bring. We're still hoping we can go sometime.

Now just today we had a letter from Mamm, telling us about a farm for rent only a few miles from their place. It is a nice big farm named Beechwood Homestead, and there's a possibility we could rent it. We're trying not to get our hopes up too high, for someone may step in ahead of us again, but it does sound exciting. It's plenty short notice, but with Daed's help in making arrangements, it could be done.

It's rather hard to be serene in the midst of all these changes, not knowing what the outcome will be. We've sent a letter to Mamm and Daed right away, but the mail seems awfully slow when we're anxious. If only we could talk to them on the phone.

Serenity Prayer

God, grant me the serenity
to accept the things I
cannot change,
The courage to change
the things I can,
And the wisdom to know the
difference.

February 21

Just one more page to fill in my diary. I guess I can say for sure now that we'll be moving to Pennsylvania, onto Beechwood Homestead! We trust that our plans won't change again, but we know that nothing in life is certain. I can't help being excited about it, for Mamm wrote that it's a nice big well-kept farm. And the best part is that we'll be close to Daeds.

We hope and pray that everything will work out for us this time, and that we can make a go of it. Meanwhile, we'll try to stay serene and live one day at a time, as

God's will for us enfolds.

I will close this journal with some of a prayer from *Prayer Book for Earnest Christians*:

O Lord God!
dear merciful heavenly Father,
you have for our illumination so kindly
let the light of heaven shine upon us.
You have also granted us this fleeting day
to be used according to your holy will,
to be lived out in godly devotion.
For these, gracious gifts of yours,
O holy Father!
we give you praise and thanks,
honor and eternal glory.

Credits and References

Miriam and Nate Mast are Dora's adoptive parents. Priscilla is her birth mother. This story is based on Miriam's Journal and on *Birch Hollow Schoolmarm*, to which *Lilac Blossom Time* is a sequel (see page 2).

In each district, the Amish have church in a house, barn, or shed every second Sunday. In between the church Sundays come the no-church Sundays, used for visiting, picnics, reading, and so on.

The Golden Gems are adapted from Charlotte Mary Yonge, translator and editor, *Gold Dust* (Chicago, 1880; reprint, Philadelphia: Henry Altemus, n.d.), a collection of devotional thoughts for a holy and happy life, translated from the French series *Paillettes d'or* (1868ff.), by Adrien Sylvain (1826–1914).

The story about the cow on the sod roof,

abridged here, comes from Norway: "The Husband Who Was to Mind the House (Mannen som skulle stelle hjemme)," in *Norske Folkeeventyr* (Christiania [Oslo], 1841–44), by Peter Christen Asbjørnsen and Jørgen Moe, translated by George Webb Dasent (1859), revised by D. L. Ashliman.

"Be sure your sins will find you out." Numbers 32:23.

The verses from the apostle Paul on marital concerns are summarized from 1 Corinthians 7:32–35.

On not calling someone a "fool," see Matthew 5:22.

God's ways are higher than ours. Isaiah 55:9.

"O holy triune God . . ." From *Prayer Book for Earnest Christians*, translated and edited by Leonard Gross (Herald Press, 1997), 36.

"Lo, children are an heritage. . . ." Psalm 127:3–5.

The wedding prayer mentioned is on pages 103–4 in *Prayer Book for Earnest Christians*.

The saying about a snowy wedding bringing riches might derive from George Herbert's line "A snow year, a rich year," in *Jacula Prudentum* (1651), no. 125.

The Amish church rule against photography is based on one of the Ten Commandments (Exodus 20:4): "You shall not make unto you any graven image. . . ."

Deuteronomy 24:5 says a newly married man should stay around home for a year, to make his wife happy.

Die Botschaft is a weekly newspaper published in Lancaster, Pennsylvania, for and about Old Order Mennonites and Amish.

God will be as a mother, brother, or friend to you; see Psalm 27:10; 68:5; 103:13; Matthew 6:9; et al.

"How Great Thou Art!" was written by Carl Boberg and translated by Stuart K. Hine.

"Man proposes, but God disposes" is from Thomas à Kempis, building on similar sayings by William Langland, Miguel de Cervantes, and Proverbs 16:9.

The Serenity Prayer is from Reinhold Niebuhr, who might have received it from Friedrich Oetinger.

The prayer "O Lord God!" is from page 18 of *Prayer Book for Earnest Christians.*

The Author

The author's pen name is Carrie Bender. She is a member of an old order group. With her husband and children, she lives among the Amish in Lancaster County, Pennsylvania.

Bender is the popular author of the Whispering Brook Series, books about fun-loving Nancy Petersheim as she grows up surrounded by her close-knit Amish family, friends, and church community. This series is for a general audience, including children.

The Miriam's Journal Series is also well appreciated by many readers. These stories in journal form are about a middle-aged Amish woman who for the first time finds love leading to marriage. Miriam and Nate raise a lively family and face life with faith and faithfulness. Bender portrays their ups and downs through the seasons, year after year.

Miriam's Cookbook presents recipes for the tasty, hearty meals of Amish everyday life. They are spiced with fitting excerpts from Bender's books.

The Dora's Diary Series, also in journal form, tells about Miriam and Nate's adopted daughter going out with the young folks, becoming a schoolteacher, and growing close to a special boyfriend. After she is married, she and her family live much of the time in places outside Lancaster County.

Herald Press (616 Walnut Ave., Scottdale, PA 15683) has received many fan letters for Carrie Bender. Readers say they have "thoroughly enjoyed" her "heartwarming" books. Her writing is "like a breath of fresh air," telling of "loyalty, caring, and love of family and neighbors." It gives "a comforting sense of peace and purpose."

Library Journal says, "Bender's writing is sheer poetry. It leads readers to ponder the intimate relationship of people and nature."

The employees of Thorndike Press hope you have enjoyed this Large Print book. All our Thorndike and Wheeler Large Print titles are designed for easy reading, and all our books are made to last. Other Thorndike Press Large Print books are available at your library, through selected bookstores, or directly from us.

For information about titles, please call:

(800) 223-1244

or visit our Web site at:

www.gale.com/thorndike
www.gale.com/wheeler

To share your comments, please write:

Publisher
Thorndike Press
295 Kennedy Memorial Drive
Waterville, ME 04901